Mary Hall McClean

Life of Francis Xavier

apostle of the Indies

Mary Hall McClean

Life of Francis Xavier
apostle of the Indies

ISBN/EAN: 9783337316433

Printed in Europe, USA, Canada, Australia, Japan

Cover: Foto ©Andreas Hilbeck / pixelio.de

More available books at **www.hansebooks.com**

FRANCIS XAVIER

THE APOSTLE OF THE INDIES

BY

M. H. McCLEAN

(*Born* 1835, *Died* 1894)

LONDON

KEGAN PAUL, TRENCH, TRÜBNER & CO., L^TD.

PATERNOSTER HOUSE, CHARING CROSS ROAD

1895

" I would the light of reason, Lord,
Up to the last might shine,
That my own hands might hold my soul
Until it passed to Thine.

" Long life dismays me, by the sense
Of my own weakness scared ;
And by Thy grace a sudden death
Need not be unprepared."

F. W. FABER.

THE Story of St. Francis Xavier's life and work has been told in these pages, as far as possible, in his own words. The following are the authorities chiefly used :

"Epistolae S. Francisci Xaverii" (Rome, 1677; and later edition, with additional letters, published Cologne, 1692).

"Epistolae Judicae" (1563).

"Rerum a Societate Jesu in Oriente Gestarum Volumen" (Cologna, 1574).

"De Vita Francisci Xavierii" (Antwerp, 1596).

"Vida, Y Milagros de San Francisco Xavier, de la Compania de Jesus, Apostol de Las Indias," Por El Padre Francisco Garcia (Barcelona, 1683).

"Lettres de Saint François Xavier," by M. Léon Pagès Paris, 1855), has also been consulted.

CONTENTS

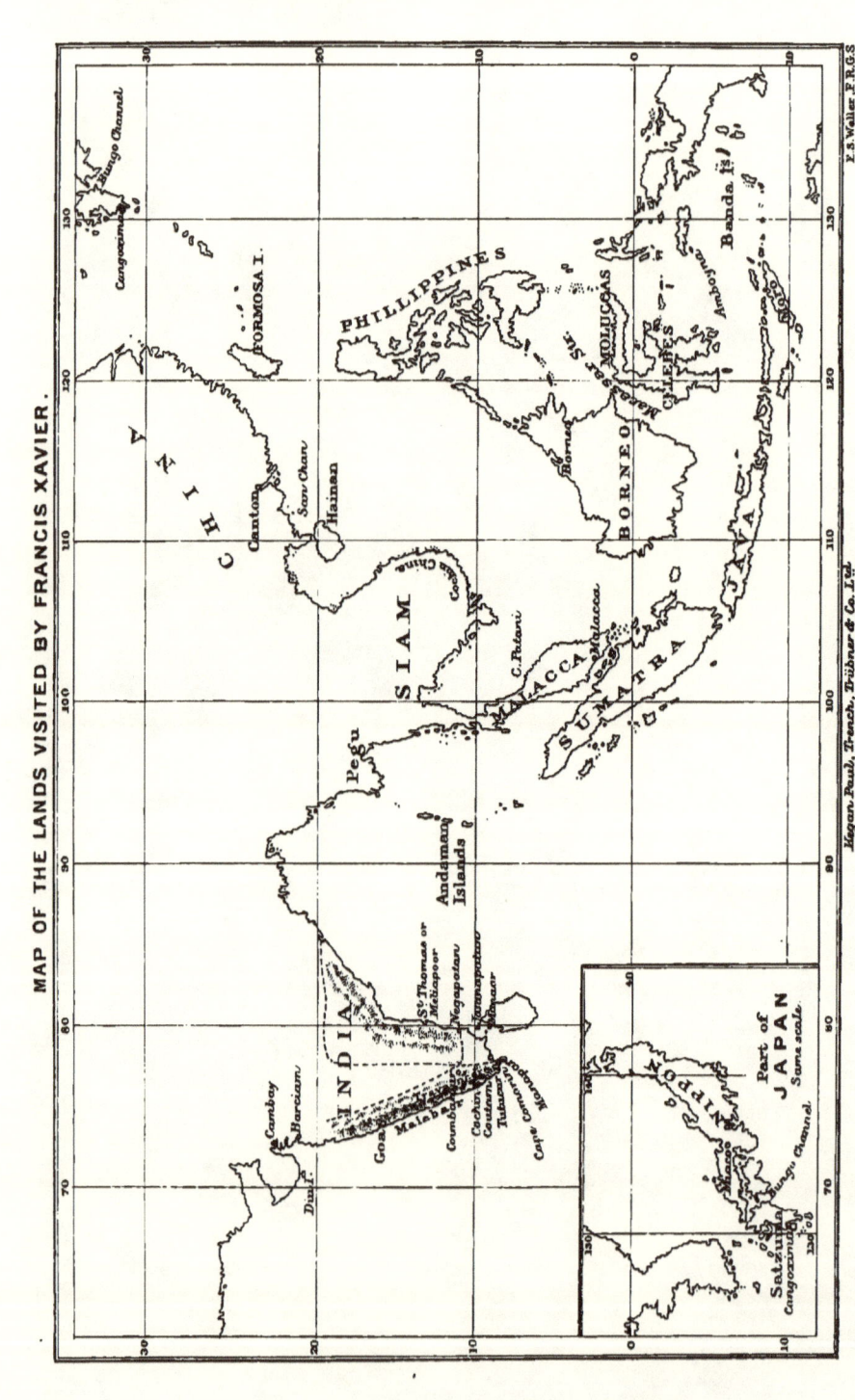

MAP OF THE LANDS VISITED BY FRANCIS XAVIER.

F.S.Weller, F.R.G.S.

Kegan, Paul, Trench, Trübner & Co. Ltd.

Part of
JAPAN
Same scale.

FRANCIS XAVIER

CHAPTER I

NAVARRE

" Glad sight wherever new with old
    Is joined through some dear home-born tie,
    The life of all that we behold,
    Depends upon that mystery."
                                                WORDSWORTH.

WE first catch a glimpse of Francis Xavier as a
studious lad, gentle and comely, well-born and well-
beloved. An old castle, old even in the beginning
of the sixteenth century, was the home of his child-
hood, not by any means a luxurious or even a cheerful one. His father, Don John Giasco, who had
acquired it by marriage with the heiress of the
Xaviers, was much absent at the Court of Navarre,
and his elder sons and daughters following him,
left the place desolate and impoverished. Only
in the remains of feudal grandeur did the Castle

A

Xavier tower above the squalid houses and narrow streets of the little town of Obanos. Yet though empty halls hung with threadbare tapestry, darkened rooms and dismal courts, formed but grim surroundings, that could not be called a gloomy abode which looked forth across the broad plain of Pampeluna, to the long range of the Pyrenees, rising tall and majestic with hoary sides and cloud-capped pinnacles. Many a day of wild sport and adventure must the boy have passed among his native mountains, bracing his nerves and hardening his frame unconsciously for the labours of his manhood—climbing the cliffs to find the eagle's nest, tracking the wolf by torchlight over the blood-stained snow, fishing for his Lenten fare in the dark lakes that lie in the heart of the hills, or rambling, on some long summer day, by pine forest and winding stream, even to where the rocky ramparts of France are cleft as with Titan sword, at the far-famed Brêche de Roland, or scaled by the sacred pass of Roncesvalles.

All the romance of the land was reality to him. Were not Roland and Charlemagne compeers of the noble Spanish Cid, himself the foremost of a long line of Christian champions, represented, even in the

boy's own day, by gallant knights, who warred
against the Moors of Grenada, or who, like Loyola,
protected the fortresses of Spain against the invading
Frenchmen ?

A missionary career seemed then a most unlikely
destiny for the young Hidalgo. His brothers were
all soldiers, scattered in the various armies of Europe,
or in those with which Charles V. was forcing Christianity upon the new-found continent of America.
It remained for the youngest son to curb the com-
bative and adventurous spirit inherent in the race,
and turn to study as his means of worldly advancement. The learned profession of the law was
chosen for him, and all his talents and energies
were early enlisted in its pursuit, although there
were many delays caused by financial difficulties,
before he was sent to receive a fitting education at
the University of Paris.

In the meantime he was left to the care of his
mother, Doña Maria d'Aspilqueta y Xavier, "a
pious and proud lady," says the old chronicler,
"devising to her son many excellent gifts of
nature, along with her own honourable name."
She brought up Francis pure in heart and fearing
the Lord, forming in him habits of self-denial and

reverence, a love of truth and sense of duty, that coloured his future life. The mother we see once again, dwelling, aged and widowed, in the same abode. Long years have passed there in peaceful monotony, while her boy has been wrestling with all the evils of the wide world that she knows only by report.

Other sons are with her now, returned from the wars, or the seas, with riches to gladden the ancestral home, and dutiful care for her comfort, while he, the youngest and the darling, is journeying in pilgrim garb across his native Pyrenees and the plain of Pampeluna, on his way to rougher mountains and more burning plains, to a homeless life and a lonely death, in the far and unknown East. Only a few short leagues separate them, yet he will not permit himself to turn from the appointed road, even to bid farewell to her he can never hope to see again on earth, but trusts to rejoin in heaven.

Female influence of a gentler type helped to mould the character of this knight-errant among saints whose chivalrous treatment of women and mothers and little children has no precedent. His Jesuit chroniclers tell us of a sister, Doña Maria

Magdalena. Beautiful and gifted, she retired from the pleasures of a Court to the convent of the poor Clares. Her prophecy of the future greatness and usefulness her brother was to attain in the East, seems to prove such intimacy and confidence between them as enabled her to share the secret aspirations of his heart, and it was by her gentle pleadings that his father was reconciled to his altered ambition.

In 1520, when he was about fourteen years old, there came into Xavier's life the man who was destined to influence him more than either mother or sister.

Ignatius Loyola was that year in charge of the town of Pampeluna—a soldier, reckless and daring, head of the inefficient garrison of that half-fortified town.

The land was at peace, the brunt of battle falling on other frontiers, when suddenly, without note of challenge or proclamation of war, French regiments came marching down upon the plain to surprise the place, and menace the independence of the little border kingdom. Any defence of the walls was impossible, but a few brave spirits made good their retreat into the citadel, and held it, in the

midst of the invaders, for many a long day, until
their leader Loyola fell, stricken as it seemed, with
his death wound.

Deprived of his persuasive counsels of self-sacri-
fice, honour and patriotism, they surrendered to the
superior forces of the enemy ; but the delay gave
time for the King of Navarre to remonstrate with
his aggressive brother of France, and obtain the
instant recall of troops that would have devastated
all the country round, had it not been for that
skilful check.

All the neighbourhood gloried and rejoiced in
their deliverance, and forgot perhaps the name of
their preserver. The feat could not fail to charm
the imagination and impress the memory of a brave
boy, dwelling within a few leagues of the spot.

Ten years afterwards Francis met his hero in Paris,
and was sorely amazed to find the undaunted captain changed into the theological student, the care-
worn ascetic, meanly clad and subdued in manner.
But, changed though he was, Loyola soon gained
a complete ascendency over the wayward youth,
whose steps he haunted like some friendly ghost,
and it was his hand that in days soon to come
rescued Francis from destruction.

CHAPTER II

PARIS

" Poor soul, the centre of my sinful earth,
　　Fooled by those rebel powers that thee array,
　Why dost thou pine within and suffer death,
　　Painting thine outward walls so costly gay ? "
SHAKESPEARE.

PARIS was a pleasant place in the days of the first Francis. A city rising into architectural beauty and literary fame, splendid with tourney and pageant, thronged with the noble and the learned of all countries, thrilling with political and intellectual excitement—court, camp, and college all in one.

The young Spaniard led a pleasant life amidst these manifold attractions, while he was yet but a student at the far-famed University ; light of heart, with steady aim and boundless ambition, enjoying, for the first time, liberty, society and success. But when, in 1530, he had completed his course with distinction, taken the degree of Master of Philosophy, and commenced reading Aristotle and teaching logic, his peace of mind was gone.

College honours are, perhaps, harder to bear than any others. A man cannot rest on these early laurels, yet it is painful to leave them and start afresh for some far distant goal. The stimulus to exertion is suddenly withdrawn, the hardworked faculties relapse into indolence, and it takes time before the talents, that learning has tested but not tried, work again. So Xavier, having attained his first ambition and engaged in learned pursuits, felt the need of some stronger excitement. He plunged into theological speculation, and distracted his soul with doubts. He rushed into gaiety and dissipation, and squandered away his slender fortune.

Pupils failed and comrades left him ; priest and Pharisee passed by on the other side ; but one friend did not forsake him. Ignatius Loyola, living at the College of Santa Barbara, striving with self-denial and mortification to make up for the wasted years of his own youth, resolved to save his young countryman. He gave him, not good advice, but sympathy and appreciation, cheerful companionship that weaned him from bad society, encouragement and support

both in public and in private. He supplied him
with funds with a delicacy that no pride could resist,
and introduced him to scholars and influential men,
whose friendship smoothed the path of ambition
before him, and the world again grew very fair.

Then, when life was bright and fortune smiled,
this faithful friend turned upon Xavier with the
solemn question : " What doth it profit a man, if he
gain the whole world and lose his own soul ? "
Xavier, ambitious and successful, turned a deaf ear
to these words, and pursued his worldly course.
Still from time to time he sought the friend to whom
he owed so much, and for whom he had so profound
an affection, and again and yet again this friend
repeated : " What doth it profit a man, if he gain
the whole world and lose his own soul ? " With
sweetness, with persistence, Loyola sought to win
this youth, whose great gifts he wished to secure
for the service of the Lord. He showed him the
vanity of all earthly success, he preached to him the
words which have resounded through the course of
ages : " What doth it profit a man, if he gain the
whole world and lose his own soul ? "

At last Xavier, touched by the patience and
insistence of his master, consented to practise the

spiritual exercises which he advised. Discipline, fasting and prayer, assisted by divine grace, prevailed, and Francis came out from his trial breathing only desire for the glory of God and the salvation of souls.

What, indeed, did it profit any man to gain the whole world and lose his own soul? What could a man do better, in this world, than win souls to God?

Boldly and cheerfully, unvexed by the doubts and backslidings that attend resolutions made in the hour of danger or despondency, Francis devoted himself to a religious life in the way that seemed clear to him; persevering in his ordinary vocation until some harder task should be found for him, and exercising himself, after Loyola's example, in fasting and meditation, penitence and prayer. Of the instability of fame and riches he had received a practical illustration, and he laid them down, as he would have laid down life itself, at the bidding of the friend whose love and patience had revealed to him something of the infinite love and patience that watches over the souls of men.

On the 15th of August, 1534, in the dark crypt of Montmartre, Loyola and his little company gathered

together for worship in the chapel dedicated to St.
Denis, the martyr Bishop of Paris. They were
only seven in number ; Loyola, majestic in bearing,
his dark eyes glowing with fervent feeling ; Xavier,
with his blue eyes and chiselled features, his buoyant
step and cheerful bearing, filled with the most
absolute faith in his leader, and with that hopeful
spirit that never forsook him under the most trying
circumstances ; Jacques Lainez d'Almazan, who ably
seconded Loyola in all his work, and who, in 1558,
succeeded him as head of the Company of Jesus,
then grown to be one of the great powers of the
Church ; Simon Rodriguez d'Azevedo, who founded
the Jesuit College of Coimbra ; and Pierre Lefevre,
who carried the work of the Company to Germany ;
and two others of less note completed the little
congregation.

Pierre Lefevre was the only priest among them,
and he celebrated Mass and administered the
Blessed Sacrament to his companions, and then
joined them in a solemn vow to renounce the world,
to keep themselves in poverty and in chastity, to
spend themselves in an absolute devotion to the
good of souls and the service of God, either in the
Holy Land or among the infidels, or in any work

the Vicar of God should appoint, without reservation, stipulation, or conditions of any kind.

Chivalrous by nature, brave, confident in their vigorous youth and powers of endurance, these founders of the Society of Jesus came to secure themselves from change by their solemn vow, and they realised that by it they bound their lives, singly so weak, into a faggot that union should make strong enough to do whatever work God might see fit to require at their hands.

Twice again these friends met in the same place and renewed their vow. Then Loyola, who had been maturing his plans meanwhile, bade them join him at Venice to prepare for their passage to the Holy Land.

So Francis must leave the fair city of Paris, now become a second home, the college where he was held in high esteem and was about to be received as Doctor of Divinity, and his quiet domicile in the tower of St. Jean Lateran. He must refuse, too, the tempting offer made him of the rich canonry of Pampeluna, which, if accepted, would have restored him to his native place in honour and prosperity. He must start in mid-winter upon travels of which no man could see the end, on foot, and begging his bread, through countries peopled with enemies and overrun with hostile soldiery. How little he shrank from these, or any other sacrifices ordered by Loyola, is shown in the letter* (the first of his preserved to us) that he wrote to his brother about this time :

"I desire greatly that you should understand how gracious God has been to me in giving me to know Master Ignatius, the most perfect man in the world. Never, in my life, can I repay the services that he has already rendered to me. Many times he succoured me in distress, and brought me friends when I first needed them, and saved me from the evil companions that my inexperience failed to detect."

* This letter is addressed to Captain Juan d'Aspilqueta at Obanos. Though not stated, it is generally referred to the year 1535, as it relates to Loyola's journey into Spain.

CHAPTER III

ITALY

" I say to thee, do thou repeat
To the first man thou mayest meet
In lane, highway, or open street—

" That he and we and all men move
Under a canopy of love
As broad as the blue sky above."

TRENCH.

THERE was a joyful meeting in the old sea-girt city of Venice between Ignatius and the friends who had followed his footsteps from afar. Not one of them was lost ; indeed, three others, fervent and faithful, had been added to their number. So ten brave souls took counsel together, concerning the conversion of the world.

Difficulties and perplexities seemed to encompass them. The Holy Land was far away and hard of access. They waited long for a possibility of reaching it, but they found work ready to their hand in relieving the misery and suffering around them. In hospital and prison they began their labours of love.

All were active, all were devoted, but in zeal and tenderness Xavier surpassed them all. To nurse those afflicted with hopeless and loathsome disease, and wait upon the mean and degraded of his race, could not have been a congenial task to a refined and educated man. Yet he did this, day and night, sparing himself neither disgust nor humiliation to give one moment of comfort or religious consolation to these poor wretches, so near death, and, for the most part, so far from Heaven. In fact, he served at the Hospital of Incurables as if there were none but incurables in the universe.

His strength lay in this singleness of aim. He left to Loyola with entire confidence, all care for the future of their Society, all subtle reasoning upon its powers and special study of its several members, all tedious balancing of conflicting calls and nice adjustment of means and ends. Counsel he gave, prompt and efficient, sympathy, from the depths of his heart ; but he obeyed now, as unhesitatingly as he commanded afterwards, and, whatever his hand found to do, he did with all his might.

His was a trusting, impulsive nature, able to fulfil to the very letter the Scriptural injunction about taking no thought for the morrow, and the little Latin hymn, ascribed to his hand, is at least in unison with the spirit that dwelt in him :

"O Deus, ego amo te !
Nec amo te ut salves me,
Aut quia non amantes te
Aeterno punis igne,
Tu, tu, mi Jesu, totum me
Amplexus es in cruce.
Tulisti clavos, lanceam,
Multamque ignominiam,
Innumeros dolores,
Sudores et angores,
Ac mortem : et haec propter me
Et pro me peccatore.

"Cur igitur non amem te,
O Jesu amantissime ?
Non ut in coelo salves me,
Aut ne aeternum damnes me
Nec premii ullius spe,

Sic amo et amabo te,
Solum quia Rex meus es,
Et solum quia Deus es.   Amen." *

The three years passed in Italy were to Francis
an invaluable apprenticeship to the business of his
life, since it is by contact, close and friendly, with
men of every class and age and calling, that abstract
human nature can alone be comprehended.   For us,

* " Oh Lord, my God, I love but Thee,
   Not for the sake of saving me,
   Nor that in flames eternally
   Who love Thee not, Thy face must flee—
   All-embracing Jesus—Who
   On the cross didst clasp me too !
   Piercing nails and spear were borne,
   Cruel, ignominious scorn,
   Agony beyond belief,
   With immeasurable grief,
   Even to death—and all for me,
   A sinful man exceedingly !

" What can prevent my loving Thee,
   Most tender Jesus ?   Not for fee
   Of high salvation, nor for dread
   Of endless judgment on my head,
   Nor hope of gain unmerited ;
   But even as Thou hast cared for me
   I love, and ever will love, Thee,
   King of my every thought and word,
   Because Thou only art the Lord.   Amen."

B

this portion of his career is the least interesting, since we have no letters written by him during the time, nor any eye-witnesses of importance, to give account of his actions, apart from the other members of the Society, whose wanderings we shall follow as briefly as possible.

They all journeyed together to Rome, to ask the Pope's benediction on their labours, were well received by Paul III. and admitted to preach before him during his meals, obtaining his entire approval and some funds towards their Mission. These they carefully reserved, subsisting while in Europe entirely upon alms.

On their return to the Venetian States, the scheme of a voyage to the Holy Land being finally abandoned as hopeless on account of the war with the Turks, they took fresh vows of poverty, obedience and chastity, at the hands of the Papal Legate. Such of them also as were not already priests were admitted to full orders, and Francis celebrated his first Mass at Vicenza with much emotion, having prepared for the holy office by months of fasting and solitary meditation.

More healthful employment for his energies was found at Bologna, where he and another were sent to preach. Scholarly attainments, polished address,

and familiarity with all the peculiar temptations
of University life, gave him immense influence
among the students, in whose manners and morals
he worked great reforms, and turned many minds
of the highest order to the service of the Church.
His host, Jerome Casalini, Rector of Santa Lucia,
seemed to have entertained angels unawares in the
enthusiasts, who roused his somnolent piety with
morning prayers and midnight meetings, street
preaching, public catechising, and prison visiting,
such as had never before disturbed the indolent
unbelief of his parish.

In 1538, Rome itself was the scene of a great
religious revival. Ten foreign priests, already
known by their success in different parts of Italy,
assembled there in Lent, pouring forth, from all
the principal pulpits, floods of impassioned eloquence that attracted crowds of curious listeners.
In the Church of St. Laurent in Damaso especially,
preached one not unknown to us. Xavier, "ghastly
and emaciated by illness and by austerities, seemed
to give his congregation warning of the solemn
certainty of death, as much by his face as his
words, while the fervour of his exhortations drew
tears to all eyes, and bore witness daily to the
power of the Spirit over mortal weakness." The

voice of dignified rebuke, of convincing argument, of earnest persuasion, gained a hearing once more in the capital of Christendom, luxurious and abandoned now as in the days of the Cæsars. The hard-hearted rich and the discontented poor, the supercilious wise and the brutally ignorant, idlers, oppressors and usurers, were alike moved by these solemn preachers to sudden repentance and visible, if sometimes short-lived, amendment. The work begun in the pulpit was continued in the confessional. These strangers, austere of morals, yet most gentle in manner, contrasted favourably with the corrupt and haughty Roman ecclesiastics, and hundreds came to them who had never sought spiritual aid before.

Loyola meanwhile was exerting every influence in organising the Society of Jesus, and obtaining its formal recognition from the Pope, and leave to include the promise of obedience to himself among its other vows. Even before the necessary formalities were completed, a request came from the King of Portugal that some of the fraternity might be sent to Lisbon to accompany an expedition designed for the spread of Christianity in the East Indies, where commerce had been hitherto the only object of European influence. The immediate interests of the Order seem to have engrossed the Founder's attention at this period, somewhat to the neglect of its first aim. He feared to diminish its prestige by separation, or to weaken its forces by division, and hesitated to despatch his best men on so perilous a mission. Especially he was unwilling to part with his dear personal friend, so that it was not until ill-health disqualified one of the two first chosen that brother Francis was called from his work in Rome to the very career that had long been the subject of his prayers by day, and his dreams by night.

" There's a Divinity that shapes our ends,
Rough hew them how we will."

One day sufficed to make preparation for the journey to the ends of the earth. He left for his benefactor Ignatius a last proof of confidence in a sealed vote for his election as Superior of the Company, and a blank subscription to all the resolutions concerning its form and discipline. Then he bade a long and sorrowful farewell to that brother of his soul, and his trusty companions, and left Rome in the suite of the Portuguese ambassador.

CHAPTER IV

PORTUGAL

" Let doctrines be.
Thou shalt be judged by thy works; so see to them,
And let divines split hairs : dare all thou canst,
Be all thou darest ;—that will keep thy brains full.
Have thy tools ready, God will find thee work.
Then up and play the man ! "

KINGSLEY.

THE journey from Rome to Lisbon occupied three months. It is perhaps to be regretted that the two letters, written at the time, do not give us some details of the style of travelling, the state of the countries traversed so leisurely, or the social as well as the religious characteristics of the ambassador Don Pedro Mascarenas and his miscellaneous following. But the Jesuits were cosmopolites from the first. The intense interest with which they studied the hidden minds of men often blinded them to mere outward peculiarities. The similarity of human beings always seems to have impressed them more than the differences, and even the black and brown varieties disturbed but little the equanimity of their contemplation. Degrees of comfort by which civilisation is unconsciously measured must have been inappreciable to bodies kept voluntarily in a state of torture, and beauty even on the face of Nature could not charm eyes that had seen cause to weep over the noblest of cities and the fairest of lands—Italy, in the golden age of Art.

So we must not expect from this intellectual, eloquent Father Francis, the gossiping chronicles by which a simple garrulous friar in like situation would carry us back pleasantly to bygone days. His eyes were in Heaven and his heart in the Indies, and nothing in Europe affected him now but the friends he had left and the work he had undertaken. Despondingly enough he writes to Ignatius from Bologna :   .

" Upon the blessed Easter Day I received your letter. The peace and consolation it brought me God alone knows. Henceforth in this life, I feel but too surely, we can only reach each other by letters, but in the other life we shall meet again, face to face, and be united in more perfect love. It remains to us only during our term of exile in the world to bestow mutual consolation by writing frequently, and in this I shall not fail you. . . . .

"I am resolved, in whatever part of the earth I may be, to remain in closest union with you and the Company at Rome, by reciprocity of letters and spiritual services. We shall send you faithful and exact accounts of all our affairs, even as children relate their doings to a mother."

The remainder of the letter is filled with what we may call professional detail upon the churches in which he preached, the number of communicants, the friendly disposition of some cardinal, and the condescension of the ambassador, ending with a message of sympathy to one Faustina Ancolina, a Roman lady, mourning apparently the loss of a murdered son. "Let her rest assured," he says, "that even in India I shall never forget to pray for her, nor for her dear Vincent, who was also mine. Already he petitions in Heaven for those who caused his death. Bid his father try to forgive them too."

The second letter, dated from Lisbon, gives a very general account of the journey, dwelling rather

upon the grace of God, in preserving all the party
from sickness, and in permitting His servant, the
writer, to minister to their spiritual advancement. He
rejoices much over the special providence by which a
head groom of the ambassador's, carried away with
his horse, in a foolhardy attempt to ford a torrent,
was tossed back upon the bank before their eyes,
in answer to their despairing prayers.

"There are a great number of people here kindly
disposed to us. Much I regret that it is not within
my power to visit and serve them all, as I could
wish ; for in many of them I find a serious inclination to good and anxiety to devote themselves to the
service of the Lord. It would be infinitely satisfactory to help them on their way to some spiritual
exercises, that might resolve them to begin, at once,
the task they postpone from day to day. A deep
conviction of their duty is, to many persons, a useful
spur, so to speak, which urges them on from seeking
rest where no peace is. Those who do violence to
their conscience, wresting the commands of God to
meet their wishes, and following their own wayward
wills rather than the inspiration of God in their
hearts, move us to deep compassion, though the

world may envy them. We seem to watch them toiling vainly up a rugged steep, where they will find but a precipice beyond, and ruin, and death eternal."

No reference is made here to his late passage of the Pyrenees, familiar as the scene must have been both to him and to his reader, nor any mention of his refusal to visit his mother on the way when pressed to do so by Don Pedro. The incident, nevertheless, is so frequently recorded that it can scarcely be without foundation.

The next fact recorded is the traveller's arrival at Lisbon, and glad meeting with Simon Rodriguez, his fellow labourer, "who was thrown into such transports of joy at beholding me once more, that the quartan fever from which he had been suffering passed its crisis, and he has experienced no return of the malady since." Then follows a description of their kind reception by the most Christian King (a just title for Don John III.), his good sense and gracious demeanour, and the important duties he had assigned them of directing the consciences of the young princes and nobles at his Court, that their influence might hereafter raise the religious standard of the whole people. " His Majesty," Xavier

adds, "is advised by some to oppose our departure
for the Indies on the ground that we may exercise
our zeal to still better purpose here; but others,
who are authorised to speak from having dwelt
many years in those countries, assure him that the
natives are all marvellously inclined to receive the
faith of our Saviour Jesus Christ, if only they be
fully convinced that the masters and interpreters
of it seek no other thing than their benefit. While
we persevere in the same frugal life and carelessness
of gain and riches and worldly advantages, abroad
as at home, these people will not hesitate to believe
our words, and we may, in a few years, convert
whole nations. At present our most useful work
seems that of seeking out, with all care and diligence,
such priests as may be willing to accompany us to
the East, with no other view than to forward the
glory of God and the salvation of man. Could we
associate ourselves with even a dozen companions
of this character, we might accomplish great things.
Already one whom we knew at Paris has promised
to come with us, and persist until death in all the
rules of our Society. Another, who is only a deacon,
offers himself with much fervour, and a doctor of
medicine, also from among our old friends, wishes

to join us and employ his healing art in spiritual interests. Above all things, we must look that those with us, no less than ourselves, are entirely free from avarice or the most distant taint of covetousness, that none may for a moment suspect that we go to conquer temporal rather than eternal possessions."

He concludes by mentioning that, at the King's desire, they were to begin preaching in public the next Sunday, though their own wish would have been to confine themselves at first to more .humble ministrations. "We shall therefore apply ourselves to the task with energy, not merely to prove our obedience to His Majesty, but because we are beholden for the goodwill borne us in this city, and are trusting in Divine assistance for the success of our efforts. We pray God without ceasing that He will increase the faith of those who come so willingly to hear any good, and show forth His mercy not for our sake, but for that of this great people, prepared to listen to us with such touching devotion. May we be enabled to comfort them greatly, and to give them understanding of the things pertaining to salvation."

We have four other letters of much the same

character despatched to Rome during the nine months that the Missionary Fathers were detained at Lisbon. Some of them appear to have been the joint production of Xavier and Rodriguez, all of them to have been intended for the perusal of the whole brotherhood, but hardly for the edification of after generations. A certain want of personality and confidential tone in them chills the reader, and makes him suspect that they contained private enclosures for Loyola of which we have no record. Those preserved are business letters. Those who cannot appreciate all Xavier's efforts and anxiety for the establishment of the Society of Jesus, nor care much for his accounts of persons and measures that contributed merely to its temporal power, may find enough to study and revere in the unwearied toil, the thought, and talent spent in the cause which he and his friends held to be the first step towards universal regeneration.

The following extracts from those letters sufficiently explain his sentiments on this and kindred subjects :

" Our souls are gladdened," he writes to Loyola on one occasion, " with the news you send us of the flourishing and prosperous state of the whole Company ; of the holy and useful labours to which you at Rome devote your time ; of the edifices, spiritual and material, which you found and finish in the sight of this and future generations, that our successors may come into possession of all things needful to continue and perfect the work now begun, with fair hope of performing signal service for our Lord. May He help us, now absent in body though present in spirit, to imitate you, whose example shows the road to follow Jesus. I, too, have news that will be grateful to you. The King, approving entirely the form of our Institute, and.perceiving already the fruit of our toil, expects much from the future. He is resolved, if our numbers multiply, to found a college as well as a residence of our Order. This excellent monarch has not been prompted by any solicitations on our part. He bears great affection to our Society, and desires its increase, like one of ourselves, guided in this, as in all things, by love and faithfulness to God. If we fail to acknowledge such obligations and confess them, according to his wishes, even in the sight of Heaven, we shall soil our souls with the vice of ingratitude, unworthy of an existence that recalls every hour the bounty of King John of

Portugal, our protector and eminent benefactor. He begs us also to keep him informed of whatever facilities the Indies afford for the conversion of their unfortunate inhabitants, showing us that his heart is full of sorrow for their wretched fate, and that he is ready to do anything, everything, to lessen the offences committed daily against the Creator and Saviour of the world by creatures formed in His image and purchased with His blood. I cannot but thank God for having permitted me to know a Sovereign at once so powerful and so pious. Were I not convinced by the testimony of my own eyes, I could scarcely credit the thought that a secular mind, dwelling amidst the tumult of a great Court, and upon the dangerous eminence of supreme rank, could be capable of such entire devotion and charity. May God increase in him these ineffable gifts, and prolong the days of a life so useful and necessary to his people.

" Paul and our Portuguese brother sail with me this week for the Indies. We go in high hopes of gathering, by the merciful help of the Lord, a rich harvest into His garner, the Church ; for we have the witness of wise men to assure us, that the very savages are ready to hear favourably the voice which shall declare to them pure doctrine, and to grasp joyfully the promises of salvation."

After speaking of the new Viceroy, in whose ship by especial favour he was to make the voyage, recounting his civilities, his good intentions and flattering predictions concerning the Mission, the writer continues :

"If persons of experience and judgment augur thus of our success, it is because they know and respect the rules of our Order, and have themselves seen the results of our ministry. For our part, notwithstanding a heartfelt conviction of weakness and insufficiency, we trust that these kind wishes and prophecies will not prove vain. We believe that God will at last take pity on the blindness and devotion even of the least of His servants in mercy to a people who know not God, but worship devils. The inmost thought of our heart is that upon the foundation of Divine aid only can we build our hopes. This support cannot fail us, on it we rest all our confidence for this immense undertaking. It is the spring of our strength, the secret nourishment of our faith. So we shall spare no efforts to succour these most miserable men, and lead them to a true knowledge of our holy religion ; keeping before our eyes the love of the Saviour, who is surely with us while we labour for His glory."

Praying the Fathers at Rome to send them advice and directions, and rules for their life and form of worship among the heathen, he still says :

"In truth we do not hesitate to avow, that actual experience must teach and guide us on many occasions, yet our principal hope of discerning perfectly the will of God, in all the conduct of the Mission, lies in counsel from you, who have hitherto been His interpreter to us. We fear to fall into the error of those who neglect to consider and weigh circumstances of place and time, and opposing interests, or who conduct themselves with pride and presumption, without listening to others, or taking the opinion of more enlightened persons, thus losing the grace and light reserved for the humble mind confessing its ignorance and weakness. Help us also, we implore you, by special petitions, in addition to your accustomed prayers, that we may have increased support in our greater need in the perils of the distant journey, and of our sojourn amidst an unbelieving race, abandoned

c

to every vice, whose pernicious influence may corrupt our frail natures, if the grace of God be not bestowed on us abundantly.

"We will write to you, at full length, by the first ships that sail after our arrival. Now, on the eve of our departure, we have no more to say, but to bid you supplicate the Lord with us, that since we have passed from you for His sake, He will reunite us all in a better world. Here it is vain to hope that we shall ever meet again, not only by the wide extent of land and waters that lies between Rome and the Indies; but because, with so great a field of promise before us, we must not, and will not, dream of the harvests of other lands, nor seek to pursue elsewhere the labours to which we have consecrated our lives."

Many efforts were made to keep Father Francis in Portugal; even the King, who had the Eastern Mission most at heart, being unwilling to part with him on its behalf.

Strengthened by Loyola's support he remained firm in his purpose, and when the winter was past, and stately galleons waited in the Tagus to convoy the new Viceroy, Don Alphonso de Soza, to the Indies, there seems to have been no longer any question as to Xavier's departure. Ceasing at last to expostulate, his royal friend dismissed him with every mark of confidence, explaining to him personally the position and circumstances of the different Portuguese colonies and military stations in India, and commending to his care both European and native subjects. Also he placed in his hands the briefs that had been forwarded from Rome, constituting Father Francis the Pope's Nuncio in all the Indies, and recommending him to David, King of Ethiopia, and other native princes on the African coast. Never any man presumed less upon favour. The royal purveyor, charged to provide him with every requisite for the Mission, declared there was more trouble in persuading him to accept a few religious books and warm garments, absolutely necessary for himself and his companions, than in satisfying the most exorbitant demands of others. When urged to take with him at least one servant, for the dignity of his office, if not for his personal convenience, he made answer that it was just such false obligations and niceties that had brought the republic of Christ's Church to its present state. For his part, he hoped to hold his place in the esteem of men by a blameless life ;

and, while Heaven granted him the use of hands and feet, to serve therewith both himself and others.

Only two companions were found ready to sail with him after all. These were Paul di Camerino, an Italian who had followed him from Rome, and young Francis Mancias, or Mansilla, described in a late letter as "an excellent creature, abounding in zeal, in virtue and simplicity, rather than in learning or science." Simon Rodriguez had been persuaded, indeed ordered, to remain behind, for the most necessary object of preparing those who were to follow, and of superintending the foundation of colleges that were to supply the world with Jesuit missionaries. Nevertheless, it was not without pangs of self-reproach that upon the day of embarkation he heard, for the last time, the confession of his more enterprising brother. With awe-struck faith he listened to visions that seemed to portend the future. "Dreams of mighty labours and endless fatigues, sufferings of hunger, of thirst, of cold, countless voyages, shipwrecks, treasons and persecutions, earthly perils and heavenly ecstasies," so intensely realised, that the sleeper had awakened with the passionate prayer : "More, more—yet more, O Lord, for Thee."

Holding solemn converse upon this and other matters, the two enthusiasts walked down together from the hospital outside the town, where they had made their dwelling among the poor of the land, through the streets and market-places of thriving, populous Lisbon to the water's edge. Then Simon turned back alone to the city, and Francis was taken on board the *St. Jago.* The anchors were weighed and the two missionaries, in company with the Viceroy and his suite, sailed away out of the shadow of the great rock, till the convent-crowned "sierra" and all the friendly shores sank beneath the horizon.

CHAPTER V

EASTWARD

" Let Knowledge circle with the winds,
    But let her herald Reverence fly
    Before her, to whatever sky
    Bear seed of men or growth of minds."

TENNYSON.

In the year 1493 of the Christian Era, Columbus, exploring for a sea-route to India, stumbled, so to speak, upon another hemisphere, part of which still bears in its name of West Indies a record of his hopes and expectations. Four years later, in 1497, Vasco di Gama, a Portuguese mariner, succeeded where many had failed before him in rounding the Cape of Good Hope. This notable voyage, scarcely less important than the other in its consequences, opened the great Indian Ocean to foreign navigation. Then the full tide of trade and colonisation swept in, and West and East met face to face. A sea voyage, however tedious, does not destroy men's nationality, alter their appearance, or impair their authority, as travels through barbarian lands are apt to do. The planks of the ship seem, in some sort, to bridge the ocean and maintain some actual connection between the mother country and her wandering sons.

The daring Portuguese, who appeared suddenly upon all the coasts of India, with their natural advantages of dress and appointments, their fire-arms, military discipline and naval skill, their greed of gold and lust of power, were not men to be despised. Wherever they set their foot the natives bowed down before them, and hastened to secure their tolerance and protection, by entering into commercial relations. They planted settlements and depôts wherever it best suited them, and insisted on immediate recognition among the ruling States. More humane, or at least more politic, than the "Conquerors" in the West, they contented them-selves with cheating instead of robbing and murder-ing the children of the soil, while the servile Hindoos submitted to their insolent assumption and sought compensation rather than revenge. Fraud was matched with fraud in place of violence with treachery, and there was no war of extermination, but hollow peace and great apparent prosperity.

The Portuguese colonies soon became a sort of Utopia to many for whom " El Dorado " had no attractions. Officers of character and talent went out to organise the government, merchants of repute engaged themselves in developing the resources of the country. A chain of maritime communication united the several stations round the peninsula of Hindostan from Cambay to St. Thomas. Goa, a central point upon the western coast, and the port most convenient to Europe, rose rapidly into a considerable city. Fortresses were built and maintained in the African harbours to protect the fleets that sailed yearly to and from Lisbon. All the neighbouring islands joined the trade in jewels and spices, and rich cargoes of silk were received from countries yet unexplored.

Only in one direction there was little progress. The sovereigns of Portugal, in obtaining from the Pope—as God's regent upon earth—rights of exclusive dominion over these far-off countries, had in fact bound themselves to provide for their spiritual enlightenment. They were to spread the faith of Christ while enlarging the borders of Christendom.

In fulfilment of this serious obligation a Bishop was appointed for Goa, and with him were sent out a few Franciscan monks and other priests of the ordinary type, without any special instructions. These good men found before them lands full of ignorance and idolatry. Amazed and inefficient, they were forced to confine their ministrations to the band of nominal Christians upon the seaboard, while on one hand lay a whole continent peopled by idolaters, and, on the other, innumerable islands inhabited by Moors or Mahometans.

Their cry of despair reached the ears of Europe, and, in reply to it, the gentle and upright John III. sent forth the Jesuit missionaries to the rescue. He gave Xavier the Pope's commission to preach the Gospel, expound the Scriptures, celebrate religious rites, reconcile heretics, grant dispensations, and regulate the affairs of the Church from the Cape of Good Hope to the utmost Indies. What practical instructions he, and probably Loyola also, may have added to these powers, is now a matter of conjecture.

Xavier's bold spirit leapt forward to his task. With visionary zeal he exulted in the wide prospect before him, to be filled with the glory of God ; while his heart strained with impatience at the thought of multitudes of human beings dying daily in the darkness that he, and such as he, had power to disperse. He must by this time have been fully aware of his own powers of influencing masses of men. Wherever he had yet preached—in Venice, Bologna, Rome, or Lisbon—he had seen the results in public amendment. The very humility with which he recognised in all this the work of the Spirit, and held himself merely an instrument in the hands of Providence, gave him greater confidence. What were difficulties of language, of position, of opportunity, to one who relied solely upon Divine aid? He had no personal fear. Suffering and privation were to him the first conditions of a godly life, and death but the final seal of its acceptance. That he was not blind to danger is evident from the tone of his last letter to the brethren, where we find him moved even to agony by the hideous tales of cruelty and iniquity that surfeited with horrors all accounts then attainable of his new sphere of labour. He spent little time in seeking the testimony of others, but strove to keep his mind unbiased, and to see with his own eyes the one step in advance which was all his faithful soul required.

It is easy to picture the huge ship, the triple
bulwarks thronged with swarthy sailors, the soldiers
marshalled upon deck, the Governor and his officers
lounging in the shadow of the slanted masts and
drooping sails, spread like wings of shelter overhead.
In the midst of this goodly company stood Father
Francis in his ragged cassock; of noble aspect,
bearing himself erect and unabashed, and grasping
his crucifix with firm hand. Beneath a brow rather
broad than high, dark blue eyes gazed searchingly
into the countenances around, and the short auburn
beard curled round most eloquent lips, as he dilated
upon the power, and the glory, and the loving care
of Him Whom the winds and the waves obey, Who
holds the seas in the hollow of His hand.

Week after week the impressive service was
continued, until the unlearned could no longer plead
ignorance, nor the frivolous forgetfulness of religious
truths and commandments, and the sick and sorrowful and forlorn, the friendless sailor and the home-sick
soldier, were cheered and strengthened by words of
love and comfort.

Nor was pleading the only way in which this faithful servant set about his Master's business. He
had "a fellowship with hearts to keep and cultivate."

Very speedily he won the goodwill of all on board, by kindly actions and ready sympathy. He was found, now closeted with the Viceroy over high schemes of government and reform, or holding brilliant discussions upon questions of scholarship or theology with the gentlemen of his suite ; now sharing the labour and the confidence of some forlorn cabin-boy, soothing the murmurs of some neglected veteran, or planning blameless amusements for the crew. Rough sailors hushed their oaths, and gambling soldiers hid their dice, on his approach ; but he looked on every innocent pastime with cheerful toleration, and was seen now and then holding the stakes to secure good-humour and fair-play, or even taking part himself at chess or other sober games. Standing aloof from every selfish consideration, he became the general arbiter upon all disputed points, and more than once his prompt and fearless interposition prevented the shedding of blood that so frequently terminates a quarrel among the fierce Southern races still retaining the blood of Moorish ancestry.

His solicitude for the preservation of life and the relief of the smallest bodily ailments is very noticeable, compared with his own recklessness in risking

infection and courting hardship, from a generous
wish to share those miseries that he could not
banish. He declined the luxuries of the Governor's
table, and lived upon the simple fare offered him as
alms, until, by reason of the length of time the ship
had been afloat, food became scarce among the
poorer passengers, and he was fain to accept the
daily portion he had before refused, not for his own
sustenance, but for the weak and famishing, whom
no man regarded. In the same spirit he converted
the little cabin appointed to his use into the general
infirmary, where he would bring, in his arms or on
his shoulders, those smitten with any disease, however loathsome, and lay them on his own bed, with
more than a brother's care ; while without, upon the
bare boards, his head pillowed upon a coil of rope,
he slept the sweet sleep of a weary child, the stormy
winds and waves cradling him never so roughly.
One writes : " It pleased God to send a great pesti-
lence upon the fleet that year, so that in the vessel
there were more sick men than sound. Day by day
the plague increased. Some ceased to breathe, others
were struck down afresh. He who stood feared ever
to fall, and none cared but for his own distress.
Death spread through the ranks of terror swiftly as

a victorious enemy through a routed army. Forgetting his own danger, afflicted with the sufferings of all, he was, as necessity demanded, doctor or nurse, father, consoler, or servant to the meanest who claimed his care. He nourished and tended those too weak even to feed themselves, and strengthened them with sweet and gracious words, counselling submission to the will of God in their infirmity, and confidence in His mercy at the hour of death. None departed from life without his hearing their last confession, and standing by to support the spirit in the extreme agony, until it passed from his arms into the hands of its Maker."

All this love, all these acts of charity, so endeared Xavier to all around, that Christians, Mahometans and idolaters alike gave him the title of Holy Father. This he was always afterwards called, and the name served to designate him to the end of his life.

CHAPTER VI

THE VOYAGE

" Then I preached Christ : and when they heard the story—
    Oh, is such triumph possible to men ?
Hardly, my King, had I beheld Thy glory,
    Hardly had known Thine excellence till then.

" Thou in one fold the afraid and the forsaken—
    Thou with one shepherding canst soothe and save ;
Speak but the word ! the Evangel shall awaken
    Life in the lost—the hero in the slave."

F. W. MYERS.

THE remaining incidents of the voyage and its happy termination are thus related by Francis himself to the brethren at Rome :

"Leaving Lisbon on the 7th April, the year of our Lord 1541, we only arrived in the Indies this sixth of May, having spent more than a twelvemonth on a journey which seldom occupies half that time. We came in the same vessel with the Governor, who treated us always with great consideration. I may add that our health has been perfect throughout. Neither have we wanted for employment in the interval, but have had confessions to hear both of sick persons and whole, while the preaching upon Sundays has never once been interrupted. What gratitude I owe to the Lord, for thus making me to meet, in the midst of the kingdom of the waters, human beings whom I have been enabled to instruct in divine mysteries and admit to the sacrament of penitence, not less needful at sea than on land!

"We touched upon our way at an island named Mozambique, where there are two fortresses, one garrisoned by the King of Portugal, the other by his Mahometan allies. There we had to winter for six months, in company with a host of people, belonging to the five other ships. Numbers of them were taken ill, and no fewer than eighty died. We abode continually in the hospital, charging ourselves with the service of the sufferers; Fathers Paul and Mancias taking heed to their present necessities, while I endeavoured to administer spiritual as well as temporal remedies, purging these unfortunate ones from their sins and making them partakers of the body of Christ. Nevertheless I, alone, could by

no means satisfy this eager multitude. Every
Sunday I preached publicly to an immense concourse
of people, brought together by the presence of the
Governor. Often also I was forced to go to receive
the confessions of persons at a distance. So the
Apostolic work went ever forward, and by the grace
of God those six months were made profitable to all.

" India lies about 900 leagues beyond Mozambique,
and the Viceroy was anxious to reach his destination with all speed, but many of his followers were
still unable to proceed, from ill-health. We therefore begged that some of us might stay awhile on
the island, to take charge of those left behind. In
deference to this request Paul and Mancias remained,
while I accompanied him, his own health appearing
so much impaired that it was desirable one should
be near to receive his confession in case of the
worst. Thus I arrived in India along with his
Highness, and expect my comrades daily by the
vessels which usually come in September.

"From Mozambique, our voyage lasted two months,
but we passed several days at Melinda, a port held
by friendly Mahometans, where the Sultan of the
country came on board, to salute the Viceroy, showing him every mark of respect and amity. Portu-

D

guese merchants frequently make a sojourn in that place, and if it happens that they end their days there, they are buried in tombs distinguished from others by crosses. They have also erected near the town a great stone cross, magnificently gilded. You will understand my joy at that sight. The power of the Cross seemed to declare itself rising thus in triumph in the midst of Mahometan dominions. During our stay, the obsequies of one who had died in the ship were performed with all the ceremonies of religion, to the great edification of the Mahometans who extolled our practices in the burial of the dead. One of the principal inhabitants of the town then asked me if the temples where Christians worshipped were generally full of believers, and if Christians were fervent and assiduous in their devotions. He himself grieved much over the lukewarmness of religion among his people, and desired to know if the case were the same with us. Of the seventeen mosques at Melinda, only three were frequented, and those by few persons. So this man, troubled in his thoughts, could not understand the weakening of religious sentiment in those around, but attributed so dire a misfortune to some unknown crime that they might have committed. After we had reasoned long upon this point, I told him that God, who is truth itself, abhors every false creed and false prayer, and was therefore making theirs to fail. I found some difficulty in explaining to him my views, which seemed very far removed from his own, when there appeared one of the Kacis or doctors, well versed in all the doctrine of Mahomet. He confessed to me that if the Prophet did not return to the earth and manifest himself among them, within two years, he should certainly renounce his faith. Thus do unbelievers and infidels lead a life of anxiety bordering on despair, and it is by God's great mercy they receive these warnings, and are, from time to time, brought out of their blindness to a knowledge of the truth.

"After leaving Melinda, we landed at Socotra, an island of about a hundred miles round. It is a wretched country, consumed by the heat of the sun, and almost without resources, yielding neither wheat, rice, millet, wine, nor any fruits. Barren and verdureless, it abounds only in dates, of which bread is made, and cattle, by which the inhabitants are mainly supported. These inhabitants are Christians in name, rather than in reality, for they are profoundly ignorant and uncultivated. The greater part know neither how to read nor write, nor do they possess any historical records; only they glory in the title of Christians, and claim to be descended from those brought unto the Lord by St. Thomas the Apostle. Crosses with lamps are to be seen in the temples, to which they repair four times a day—at dawn and afternoon, sunset and midnight; the worshippers being assembled, not with bells, but with wooden rattles, such as are used at home in the holy week. Every village has its Kacis, who takes the place of a priest, though he cannot read or write any more than the rest, and has no books, but recites a few prayers from memory. They do not themselves understand these prayers, which, in fact, are in an unknown tongue, the Chaldean, I am led to suppose, with a word resembling our Alleluia repeated frequently. The Kacis never baptize any one, but are absolutely unacquainted with the sacred rite.

"Whilst at Socotra, I christened a number of children, to the lively joy of their parents, who, for the most part, evinced the greatest anxiety to bring them to us. These poor folks offered us generously of all their possessions, and such was their good-will, that I should have feared to refuse even a few dates, pressed upon me in a spirit so friendly. They besought me earnestly to abide with them, engaging that every creature in the island would come forthwith to be baptized. I also desired of the Viceroy that he would suffer me to remain in a country where the harvest of the Lord was thus ready for the reaper; but he denied my suit, fearing lest I should be carried away for a slave, since the island has no Portuguese garrison and lies exposed to the depredations of the Turks. I was on my way, he assured me, to other Christians who needed spiritual aid and instruction, no less than the Socotrians, perchance more, and among whom my efforts would be better bestowed.

"Of the five vessels left behind at Mozambique, one noted for its great size and laden with precious merchandise suffered shipwreck, the crew only escaping with their lives : the others arrived safe and sound at Goa, where we have now been five months.

"The capital of the Indies is a magnificent city with a large Christian population. It contains a Franciscan convent and a fine cathedral with full chapter, besides several other churches. We may well be thankful to find the name of the Lord held in honour, so far away in the midst of heathendom.

"I have taken up my abode in the hospital, the more conveniently to administer the Sacraments to the sick, but there are so many other confessions to be heard, that were I in ten different churches, I should have penitents enough. This work once accomplished, and the prisoners also visited, I transfer myself to the Church of St. Mary, near the hospital, where I have begun to instruct the children assembled there sometimes to the number of three hundred or more, teaching them their prayers, the Creed, and the Commandments of God. The same thing is now done in the other churches by ordinance of the Bishop of Goa. The results are more important than you can possibly imagine, and are acknowledged through the whole town.

"After preaching to the people in general upon Sundays and holy days, I explain to the natives the articles of belief, in the midst of a congregation greater than the building can well contain. Then I make them learn the Lord's Prayer, and the Angelic Salutation, the Creed of the Apostles, and the Ten Commandments of Divine Law. I also celebrate a Mass for the lepers, whose hospital is without the town, and hear their confessions and admit them to he partakers of the body of the

Lord. There were none there who approached not
to the sacred mysteries, and having heard me but
once from the pulpit, these afflicted ones manifested
an eagerness truly admirable.

"Under orders from the Viceroy, I depart shortly
for a place where there is promise of many converts
—Cape Comorin, about two hundred miles from Goa.
I am taking with me three young men of the country,
two of whom are deacons understanding Portuguese
besides their own language ; the third has only
received the minor orders. Also Paul and Mancias
are to be sent to rejoin me as soon as they shall
arrive from Mozambique. My labours there will not,
I am persuaded, be lost to the interests of religion,
and I trust that God, moved by your prayers, may
deign to forget my sins and grant me abundant grace
to serve Him worthily before the people.

"The fatigues of a long sea voyage, the heavy
charge of other men's sins, while the soul sinks
beneath its own burden, the weariness of exile in
a heathen land beneath a burning sun, are trials
that, borne for the sake of the Lord, as is our
bounden duty, become a source of spiritual comfort
and joy unfathomable. I am filled with the thought
that true followers of Christ find their happiness

in a life of trial and suffering; that to fly from the cross, or to be deprived of it, would be in their eyes actual death. Can there in truth be a more cruel death than to live without the Saviour after having tasted His love, to lose Him by seeking after one's own desire? Verily no cross is to be compared to such misfortune. It is sweeter to die daily mortifying every inclination, that we may follow, instead of our own will, the will of Jesus Christ.

"In the Lord's name I conjure you, my honoured brothers, to give me tidings of every member of our Company. Never more shall I behold them in the flesh, face to face, as the Apostle says, let me at least behold them in the Spirit by means of your letters. Do not deny me this grace for all my unworthiness. Remember that God has so placed you that I have the right both to ask and receive from you abundant support and consolation.

"Point out to me, I pray you, the course of conduct I should pursue to serve Christ among the Pagans and Mahometans to whom I am sent. My trust is that God will discover to me through you the true means of bringing them speedily into the bosom of the Christian Church. If I err in this matter your letters will correct me, and I shall endeavour to reform my practice. Nevertheless, I fear not to repose much confidence in the merits and intercession of our holy Mother Church, and the prayers of her living members, among whom you are numbered, that Jesus will proclaim His Gospel throughout the land of the infidel even by the mouth of His unworthy servant. If indeed the meanest of His creatures be employed for so great a ministry, it will abash and bring to confusion some whose vocation calls them to all high enterprises, and will encourage many a lowly spirit. Let them consider this man, who is but dust and ashes and the poorest of mortals, as a witness of the scarcity of labourers in the Indies. I am ready to become a servant, even for all my days, to such as will consecrate their strength to planting in this soil the vine of our Father.

"Here I make an end of writing, supplicating God in His infinite mercy to admit us one day into His perfect bliss, for which also we had our birth; and to increase our strength in this life, so that serving Him with the zeal He requires we may be found conformable, always and everywhere, to the decrees and inspirations of Providence.

"Goa, the 18th of September, A.D. 1542.

"Your unprofitable brother in Jesus,

"FRANCIS DE XAVIER."

CHAPTER VII

PORTUGUESE INDIA

"And is there care in Heaven, and is there love
  In heavenly spirits for those beings base,
That may compassion of their evils move?
  There is :—else much more wretched were the case
Of men than beasts. But oh ! th' exceeding grace
  Of highest God that loves His creatures so,
And all His works with mercy doth embrace,
  That blessed angels He sends to and fro,
To serve to wicked man, to serve His wicked foe ! "

SPENSER.

ARRIVED at Goa, the newly appointed Nuncio made it his first care to seek audience of the Bishop, and, prostrating himself before his superior in the Church, humbly to ask licence for the exercise of his calling within the diocese. This act of graceful, well-timed courtesy, greatly impressed Dom Joam d'Albuquerque, a prelate of excellent dispositions, though unhappily not a man of action like his relative the famous Christian

conqueror of the Indies. He raised up the sup-
pliant, to whom privation and anxiety already lent
a venerable appearance, assuring him of perfect
independence and admitting him at once into close
friendship and confidence. The Franciscan brothers
of the monastery, already established at Goa, be-
trayed more jealousy of the stranger, whom they
suspected, not without reason, of being sent to over-
look their proceedings.

Francis wisely and warily abstained from giving
cause of offence. Keeping secret for a time the
authority conferred on him by the Pope and aiming
only at moral ascendency, he sought to remedy
rather than censure their errors, to guide not to
govern their way of life ; while his personal energy
drove them to wholesome emulation, and his temper
and patience quelled the professional rivalries that
have often made shipwreck of great and holy enterprises. In a little while the whole moral aspect of
the settlement was changed, as far as human means
go, by the exertions of one man. Order and decorum
began to prevail over drunkenness and profligacy.
Deeds of flagrant injustice, violence, and dishonesty
became fewer day by day. The voice of kindness
and mercy made itself heard, and religion raised

the hymn of penitence and thanksgiving once
more. Like the surf that beats incessantly round
their island city, the words of the preacher assailed
the consciences of the mammon-seeking merchants
of Goa, with the old ever-pertinent question :
" What shall a man give in exchange for his soul ? "

A dialect of corrupted Portuguese, intelligible to
all who heard, was made, in spite of scholarly pre-
judice, the medium of vivid eloquence, mournful
satire, indignant rebuke and loving exhortation,
that riveted the attention of both European and
Hindoo ; while, sweeping over the follies and
vices of each section of the community, it recalled
them to the sacred obligations of their common
faith and led them to all things lovely, honest, and
of good report.

The new priest taught diligence and frugality by
example, and charity in its widest sense. The very
lepers had a claim upon his attendance, the needy
and oppressed found him ever at their service. At
the hospital he was a helpful inmate, at the prison
a cheering guest. Always mindful of the interests
of humanity, he introduced into the management
of both measures of care and gentleness hitherto
untried ; sending rich penitents to prove their

sincerity by alleviating mortal misery in the former, and imposing as a religious duty upon the Governor a weekly visit to the latter, that he might hear in person the prisoners' complaints and distribute even-handed justice to native and foreigner alike.

But the teaching of the children was the main feature in his ministry, as in that of his European brethren ; for ragged schools are by no means a recent invention. Francis Xavier especially is represented as walking through the streets and market-places with a little bell in his hand, crying out : "Send your children, all Christian subjects, your sons and your daughters and your slaves, that they may learn the lessons of holiness and the love of the Lord." The little ones flocked after him, and he led them by hundreds to the church, and related to them in few and solemn words the story of the Saviour's love. The warm, youthful imagination seized the loving truths, and words of prayer and praise echoed from infant lips in many a godless household.

The same system was pursued by the good Father among the native converts about Cape Comorin, whither he was despatched on a sort of missionary reconnoitre not many months later. Indeed, he seems to have been able to do little else at first than travel from village to village, baptizing numbers of unconscious babes, and giving religious instruction to the older children. " Who," he says, " suffered me neither to proceed with divine service, nor to eat, nor to rest, until I should have taught them their prayers. Now I perceive in truth that the kingdom of Heaven is of the little children, and those like unto them. To refuse their just demand would have been to offend against the Almighty, so I began forthwith to teach them a confession of faith in God the Father, Son, and Holy Spirit, also the Apostles' Creed, the Pater Noster, and the Ave Maria.

" I recognise in them wonderful intelligence, and, were there any to train them up in religion, doubt not but that they might one day become excellent Christians."

The Hindoo parents, not hard of heart though slow of understanding, were perfectly satisfied with the arrangement by which the children became in a manner their sponsors, most of them, we are told, being in time reformed by the agency of the little disciples, who were henceforth educated according to Christian principles.

St. Francis believed the heathen gods to be verit-
able devils, and held himself prepared to do battle
with them valiantly for the possession of any human
soul. Frequently, in visions, he seemed to encounter
them and prevail over them, not without bitter
wrestlings. Whatever hindrances were put in the
way of the Gospel, whatever misfortunes of storm,
or famine, or sickness befell those who heard it, he
ascribed with intense conviction to infernal agency.

This was strikingly exemplified in one of the
villages he first visited, where the inhabitants,
being all Pagans and subject to an infidel Sovereign,
absolutely refused to hear him preach. He would
not be prevented, however, from offering up prayers
for a poor woman in her last distress, on whose
behalf all the native deities had been importuned
in vain. "I began," he says, "to invoke the name
of the Lord with faith, forgetting that we were in
a strange land. I recalled these words: 'The earth
is the Lord's and the fulness thereof, the universe and all that dwell therein.' Afterwards, by
the aid of an interpreter, I strove to explain to
her the first truths of religion. Through God's
mercy she was enabled quickly to believe, and,
asked if she would become a Christian, replied:

'Yes, right willingly.' Then, repeating Gospel words never before heard in that place, I baptized her solemnly. What need I say more? She was at last delivered of a son, having trusted in the Saviour. The fame of that miracle that our God had worked in that house spread immediately through all the village. I myself went before the chiefs to signify to them in the name of the Lord that they must needs confess Jesus Christ, His Son, the Saviour and preserver of all mankind. Still they would not renounce the worship of their forefathers without at least permission from their Sovereign. I appealed to the Minister of that prince, who was fortunately then in the neighbourhood collecting taxes due to his master. When this person had heard me discourse upon our holy faith, he declared his entire approval of it, and authorised all who would to join us; but though he gave for others wholesome counsel, he forbore himself to take advantage thereof. Then the great men of the place hastened to make profession of Christianity with all their families, and the people followed the example of their chiefs, until all of every age and condition had received baptism."

What provision was made for the further instruction of these new members of the Church Catholic, stands recorded in no written document, but we may rest assured that the faithful pastor did not forget his flock in the wilderness, nor fail to send them guidance in the path he had opened to them.

Nothing ever moved him to deeper compassion than the forlorn and spiritually destitute condition of the poor pearl-fishers of Cape Comorin, who had been converted, almost first among the people of the Indies, by the Portuguese, then left for years without priests or teachers, exposed to the hatred and persecution of their infidel neighbours. Only when they were reduced to the last extreme of misery, the Saracens having carried off the boats, upon which they depended for the means of subsistence, were any European sympathies awakened on their behalf. The Viceroy armed a fleet for their defence, and overtaking the spoiler with signal vengeance, reclaimed the stolen boats, captured those of the enemy, and bestowed them also on the distressed fishermen. Naturally interested in the people he had befriended, he followed up his generosity by other marks of favour; the greatest that of deputing his confessor to inquire into their spiritual needs, and establish in their country the worship of the one true God.

E

This mission, suggested doubtless by his own good counsel, was accepted by Francis with sanguine zeal. To other eyes the post seems a less important one than was due to his talents and distinction, but to reclaim the lowest specimen of humanity was a task worthy of the noblest that walk the earth, and he undertook it in thorough earnest; not guessing, perhaps, how well it was for him to have this opportunity of familiarising himself with Eastern character, of hearing native tongues and sounding the native intellect, before entering upon any more conspicuous field of action. On foot, beneath the burning sun, and alone, save for the two or three Christian converts who accompanied him, at once as guides, interpreters and assistant priests, he made royal progress through some thirty villages, arriving at last at Tutucurin, a coast town of importance, still visible to us upon the map of India, on the eastern side of Cape Comorin. After remaining there a few months, he appears to have retraced his steps, either, according to previous arrangement to report on a province deemed too barren for Portuguese occupation, or driven by unforeseen exigencies to seek in person supplies and supporters adequate to his designs.

In the autumn of the same year we find him

again at Goa, writing to Loyola the following account of the college in which he had from the first taken so warm an interest, that he has been sometimes erroneously credited with its foundation:

"Some persons, visibly animated by the Spirit of God, have founded, very lately, a college at Goa; the thing of all others most necessary for these countries. We may all thank God in beholding the daily progress of the establishment destined to secure the education of many neophytes, the conversion of many infidels. The principal men in the town preside over its construction, and the Viceroy regards it with especial favour, so convinced of the service that it may render in the propagation of the faith, that he is completing and enlarging it with his own funds. The church belonging to it is admirably designed. The foundations are laid, the walls already rise to the coping, it will be roofed in immediately, and in the course of next summer consecrated for divine worship. To give you an idea of its size, I must tell you that it is twice as large as the church of the Sorbonne at Paris.

" This college is already endowed with revenues amply sufficient for the support of our scholars, and they will be augmented, we presume, in time. Under God's blessing, we trust that in a few years it will send forth numerous graduates, to serve the cause of religion in these lands, and extend in every direction the dominion of our holy Church. We have even now more than sixty children well prepared under the care of the excellent Diego di Borba, of the order of St. Francis, who, as soon as they are old enough, will transfer them to the college. Judging from the beginning, I hope by the end of half a dozen years to find here upwards of three hundred students of all races, of all nations, of all languages, whose future labours will infinitely multiply the number of Christians in the world.

" The Viceroy has been corresponding with the King on this subject in order that His Majesty may deign himself to write to the Pope, asking of him other members of our Company for the Indies to become the props and pillars of this institution, called by some the College of St. Paul's Conversion, by others that of the Holy Faith. To me, the latter name appears most convenient, since its sons are destined to scatter among the unbelievers the seed of Christian faith. By His Grace's command, I am to explain to you also the first object of the establishment—to nurture in the principles of Christianity native children from various parts, that, after having acquired a sufficiency of learning, they may be sent home to enlighten their own people. My words can hardly express to you how entirely the great man approves of our Order. He is fully persuaded that, as you have been the means by which we all have been called of God to be followers of the Son, he can only fulfil his own obligations by your aid, and would show you, by letter, the extreme need of good instruction for the students of the college, that you may feel bound to send members of our Company for its behoof. It is his part, he says, to finish the material edifice, and yours to build it up in piety and learning, furnishing it with eminent masters for the guidance of youth.

" He expects, then, three priests and a master of humanities to help us. I trust that one at least, if not all, will be of distinguished wisdom and virtue, for our Fathers, having at the same time to take the direction of the schools and to endure the excessive discomforts in which this country abounds towards missionaries, will be peculiarly tried in strength and courage. The ministry is such that it demands a sturdy frame and the vigour of youth, and will better suit young men than those who are past the prime, although older persons, if active and strong, might equally render good service. All who come will be received with joy and kindness by every member of the college, and speedily appointed to assist in hearing confessions, giving the spiritual exercises, and preaching in public. Assuredly theirs will be a ripe and abundant harvest.

"Your choice will also, the Viceroy hopes, include a preacher capable of unfolding the Holy Scriptures and the doctrine of the Sacraments, with all else that ought to be thoroughly understood, to the priests who come to us, for the most part, sadly wanting in knowledge. At the same time he must be careful to strengthen them in love of God and charity to their neighbours, which, doubtless, he should do by example as well as by exhortation. You, at least, know that deeds speak more persuasively than words. The others of our fraternity will be required to devote their zeal to the service of the churches, and the conversion of infidels. Even in this little island of Goa there is much yet to be done; there are numbers of men, untaught, uncared for, dwelling in the shadow of darkness and superstition, strangers to the very existence of their God and Creator."

Another letter, written about this time to his friend Simon de Rodriguez, then in charge of the Jesuit College at Coimbra, shows how bitterly Francis felt the disgrace which sullied the European rule in India by the flagrant dishonesty practised in every office.

"Do not permit," he writes, "any friend of yours to be sent to the Indies, with charge or control of His Majesty's financial affairs. It is surely of persons engaged in such business that we find it written: 'They shall be blotted out from the book of the living, and their names shall not be inscribed among the just.' Believe me, however great your confidence in men you know and love, you will do well to oppose them in this matter, to strive with all your might that they may be shielded from such extreme danger. Otherwise, unless they indeed be confirmed in God's grace, even as were the Apostles themselves, do not hope to see them persevere in their duty, or preserve their upright-ness. There is a power, all but irresistible, waiting to drag them down and overthrow them. The prospect of gain soon allures them. The facility of the prey entices them on. Their cupidity will increase with the satisfaction of their desires. Evil precedents and customs will pour down upon them like a torrent and overwhelm them, and sweep them along to the end. The idea of crime and disgrace ceases to attach itself to dishonesty, when it becomes the universal habit. There are few questions as to the lawfulness of that which is known to go unpunished. Everywhere and for ever we see goods seized by violence, and treasure heaped up, to be carried home to another country. Possessions once taken are never restored, and who can enumerate all the artifices of plunder? I am continually amazed to behold, besides the ordinary forms of theft, the various modes in which an avaricious and cruel ingenuity conjugates the verb 'to steal' with a thousand irregularities heretofore unknown."

But we are forestalling events. It was in all good faith that our missionary now took counsel with the representative of royal power concerning matters that lie near the heart of every true governor of men—public education and established religion.

Devoted priests, faithful interpreters, patient teachers, were urgently needed for the new Christians at Comorin ; but of such there was no superfluity at Goa, and the Bishop and others were anxious to keep, rather than to spare, all who could be really useful. Paul di Camerino and Francis Mancias had, however, arrived during their leader's absence, and were ready to second him in every undertaking with entire unanimity of thought and action—that grand secret of success discovered anew by the Jesuit Fathers amidst the distractions of a discordant age. After much anxious con-sultation with the authorities, civil and ecclesiastical, it was decided that the seminary and the mission must support, not rival, each other, since they were equally necessary to the progress of the faith. Paul was left behind at Goa, as Simon had been left at Lisbon, to make good the foundations by training a younger generation to follow in the footsteps of the brethren ; while Francis, accom-panied by young Mancias, Joam d'Artiaga, a Portuguese, two native priests and several lay coadjutors, embarked again for Cochin, the first station of the pearl fishery, an island on the west side of Cape Comorin off the coast of Travancore.

CHAPTER VIII

THE PEARL FISHERY

"I stand amidst the roar
Of a surf-tormented shore,
And I hold within my hand
Grains of the golden sand.
O God, can I not grasp
Them with a lighter clasp?
O God, can I not save
One from the pitiless wave?"

EDGAR POE.

Francis Xavier to the Company at Rome.

"COCHIN, *Jan. 15th*, 1544.

"IT is now three years since I left Portugal, and I write to you, my brethren, for the third time, having received but one letter of you—God knows how my soul was refreshed thereby.

"Dom Paul, Francis Mancias, and myself also, are in the enjoyment of perfect health. The former labours yet at Goa, fulfilling with admirable zeal his ministry as Rector of the College of the Holy Faith. The latter abides with me amidst the Christians of Cape Comorin, whereof the numbers are already considerable, and increasing every day.

"So soon as I arrived here I began to question the people whether they knew aught of the Lord Christ, but to all my inquiries upon the points of their belief, or concerning that which they held, being yet infidels, they answered me one thing only : that they were Christians, and that their ignorance of the Portuguese tongue alone hindered them from comprehending the mysteries and precepts of the faith. As I spoke Spanish, and they Malabar, so that they understood not my speech and theirs was unknown to me, I made choice of the more intelligent among them, and sought out carefully such as had some knowledge of both languages. Then, communing together for many following days, we succeeded by our united efforts, and not without infinite pains, in producing a translation of the Catechism in Malabar. Having committed this to memory, I began to traverse the villages of the neighbourhood, collecting both young and old by the sound of my little bell, and twice a day rehearsing to them the

Christian doctrines. Within a month the children were able to repeat it all perfectly, and I bade them teach the same to their parents, their servants, and their neighbours. On Sundays I assemble, in the house of God, men and women, boys and girls, all coming with gladness and full of the desire of instruction. In their presence I recite aloud the profession of faith in the Holy Trinity, the Lord's Prayer, the Angelic Salutation, and the Apostles' Creed, all in the language of the country ; the people following my words, and seeming to do so with pleasure. Then I take up the Creed again, dwelling upon each separate article and questioning my hearers if they unhesitatingly believe it. With firm voice and hands crossed upon the breast every one confesses aloud his Faith. I make them repeat the Creed more frequently than the prayers, showing them that it is those who believe all that it contains who are called Christians. After an explanation of the sign of the cross, I teach them the Ten Command-ments, wherein they have the sum of all Christian law, and may rest convinced that he who observes them all faithfully, is in practice and reality a Christian, assured of salvation, while he who neglects any one of these precepts, is a bad Christian, and in danger of the pains of hell, unless his sin be washed away through sincere penitence. Both neophytes and pagans are amazed at these teachings, and admire the purity of the Christian law, its perfect consistency, and accord with reason. Some principal prayers are next learned and repeated after the creed, accompanied by a short invocation in the native tongue : ' Jesus, Son of the living God, give us grace to, believe entirely, to that end we offer up the prayer ordained by Thee.'

" Thus I accustom them to petition for grace in the ordinary forms of the Church, often assuring them, that in obtaining this they will receive other gifts very abundantly, even beyond their desires. I make all, especially those about to be baptized, repeat the general confession, and I question them upon their faith, to ascertain whether they truly believe. Upon their formal profession I deliver an exhortation in their own language, explaining briefly the great truths of Christianity and the duties of such as would be saved. Only after this manner of preparation do I admit any to the rite of baptism.

" The multitudes that press forward to enter the fold of Christ are indeed so great that my hands are oftentimes wearied with baptizing them. In a single day I have thus blessed whole villages, and have persevered until strength and voice failed me, in signing the cross and repeating the prayers. None can tell how great profit there is in the baptism of infants and the instruction of children, as well as of people of ripe age. I myself have full confidence that these young converts will, by the Grace of God, prove far better than their fathers. Already they show an ardent affection for the divine law, a marvellous zeal in studying and in imparting to others religious learning. Imbued early with the hatred of idolatry, they stoutly oppose heathenism, and rise up against the idol-worship which still prevails among their families. When I find in any place sacrifices offered to false gods, I lead thither the children of the land, who heap upon the demons insult and reproach, greater than the honours their elders have rendered, and rush upon the images, overthrowing them, breaking them, and treading them under foot.

" For four months I had dwelt in a Christian town, engaged in translating the catechism, &c., when natives began to come from all parts, beseeching us to enter their houses and invoke God over the beds of the sick. At the same time so great a number of

sufferers were brought to us that I was hardly able
to repeat a gospel for each. Nevertheless we forsook not our daily duties, the instruction of children,
the baptism of those already taught, the translation
of the catechism, controversies upon difficult questions proposed to us, and the burial of the dead.
Yet my anxiety was to satisfy the desires of the
unfortunate creatures who sought our prayers for
their sick, and seeing so many come to plead the
interests of others, I feared to let their confidence in
our holy religion fail, and judged myself guilty in
refusing their reasonable request. So, as the concourse increased and I could myself neither minister
to all nor deny any, I chose out children to send in
my stead to such places as I was unable to visit.
In the chamber of the sick, they assemble the relations and neighbours, reciting with them the creed
and giving encouragement to a sure trust in the
Lord. Then they repeat the solemn prayers of the
Church, and, need I tell you, that often the faith and
piety of these little ones has restored health to the
body as well as to the soul. Wonderful providence
of God, that calls men through suffering to salvation,
bringing them, as it were, by force to the faith of
Christ!

" The same children are also able to go from house to house, through the streets and public places, charged with teaching the very ignorant some plain rudiments of Christian knowledge ; therefore, when this matter is sufficiently forwarded in one village, I myself pass on to the next, there to pursue a like course. So I visit in succession every part of the country, and, when that is accomplished, begin again my journey, taking the villages in the same order. At each place I leave a summary of the Christian doctrines, to be copied by such as can write, and learned by heart and repeated daily by the others. It is likewise ordained that all should meet together upon holy days to go over the elements of the faith in public, and catechists duly instructed have been appointed to preside over these exercises in the thirty Christian villages of the land, Dom Martin Alphonso di Soza, Governor of the Indies, having, out of regard for us and zeal for religion, assigned a sum of 4000 gold pieces for the support of native teachers.

" Infinitely greater numbers might be converted in India were it not for the pressing want of missionaries. Often I long to present myself before the Universities of Europe, that of Paris above all,

raising my voice everywhere, and crying aloud to
the learned doctors whose science exceeds their
charity : 'Behold this innumerable throng of human
souls losing heaven, falling into eternal misery
through your neglect ! ' Would to God that some of
our fine scholars might apply the same zeal to the
saving of souls as to the storing up of worldly
wisdom, rendering to God a just account of the
talents He has committed to their keeping ! Who
can tell whether a few, moved by this thought, would
not give themselves to spiritual meditation, that they
might hear the voice of the Lord in their own hearts,
and be enabled to renounce temporal vanities and
fulfil their vocation, according to that divine counsel ?
From the depths of their being they would cry :
'Here am I, Lord ! Send me whither Thou wilt,
even to the Indies.' My God, how much happier
would be their life ! How much surer their salvation ! With what confidence in the Divine Mercy
would they await their last hours, and repeat joyfully
the words of the servant of the Gospel :—'Lord,
Thou didst give me five talents, and behold I have
gained other five also.'

"If the days and nights they consecrate to the
pursuit of earthly knowledge were given to solid

F

and abiding wisdom, if the energy they display in penetrating the secrets of science were spent in teaching the ignorant the things pertaining to salvation, they would be better prepared to give account to their master. I fear that some of the divines who devote themselves to the liberal arts in our colleges think more of the honours and insignia of the priesthood than of its holy functions, to the sacred burden of which these are but witnesses. The thing has come to this, that the most renowned scholars and the greatest geniuses persuade themselves that they are seeking ecclesiastical dignities solely for the advancement of learning and the service of religion. Benighted ones who will not perceive that their learning is turned to their own profit rather than to any Catholic interest! Fearing that God should baulk their ambition, they suffer not Providence to direct their steps. Heaven bears me witness that I am almost resolved, if I return not to Europe, to write to the University of Paris, that it may know how many millions of unbelievers might with ease be brought to the faith of Christ if there came among them a sufficiency of evangelical labourers, who, forgetting themselves, should seek only the glory of God. Oh, my best beloved brothers, pray ye the

Lord of the harvest that He send labourers into His fields !

" There is a certain class of men in these countries called Brahmins, who preside over the worship of the pagan gods, perform various ceremonies in the temples, and guard the idols there. Nothing can be more perverse, more abandoned than this race. To them I apply the words of David : ' Lord, deliver me from this sinful generation, from the perfidious and wicked men.' They are given up to falsehood and imposture. With all subtlety they seek to take advantage of the simplicity of the people. They declare publicly that the gods have need of certain offerings in the temples, namely, such things as they themselves desire, for their own consumption and that of their wives, children and servants. They continue to persuade the ignorant that the images live and eat like ordinary men, so that some devotees present, even twice a day, food or money. Then, these Brahmins make good cheer with a sound of musical instruments, and say to those without that it is the gods holding festival. If provisions fail, they denounce the anger of the gods upon the people who have not brought all that was demanded of them ; nor do they hesitate to proclaim that, if they

be not speedily satisfied, the country will be plagued
with wars and diseases, and the visitations of evil
spirits. So the poor, ignorant savages are terrified
into blind obedience. The Brahmins have themselves
only a shadow of learning, but supply the want of it
by cunning and malice. They are very wroth to see
me discover their frauds. When conversing with me,
in the absence of witnesses, they plead that the idols
are their sole patrimony, since by them and by their
own lies they gain their living. They acknowledge
that I, imperfect as I am, know more than them all
put together. They salute me and offer me presents
continually, and appear much hurt at my refusal
of their gifts, but this they do to beguile me and
make me an accomplice in their frauds. They profess also to be aware that there is one God only and
even offer to supplicate Him in my favour. And I,
in gratitude for all this, reveal to every one the truth
about them. As far as in me lies, I unmask, before
the eyes of the multitude, the dark superstition
which binds them to these impostors, their illu-
sions and their falsehoods. Many of the people,
convinced by my arguments, have now abjured
the worship of idols and hastened to become
Christians—but for the opposition of the Brahmins

the whole nation would ere this have embraced the
religion of Jesus."

Such being the writer's position towards the
followers of Brahm, considerable courage was
displayed in his frequent visits to the pagodas, for
the avowed purpose of confuting the arguments of
any who would come forward to defend their time-
honoured creed. Upon one occasion he put to the
priests, in the presence of more than two hundred
worshippers, a searching question as to the duties
enjoined upon them by their gods for the attainment
of a blessed existence. None were ready to answer,
but at last a very aged and venerable Brahmin spoke
for all, asserting as their highest duties to abstain
from killing cows, since the deities were adored
under that form, and to give presents to the priests !
Moved with horror at their abject ignorance the fearless intruder rose up in the midst, demanding to be
heard in his turn, and, with a fire and vehemence
that startled the recumbent sages from their slum-
bering meditations, declared to them the one true
God and His commandments, discoursing of heaven
and hell and judgment to come till his hearers
sprang to their feet, confessing with loud accord,

that the God of the Christians must be indeed the
Lord, since His law was righteous and His command-
ment reasonable. Having convinced them also of
the immortality of the soul, and answered foolish as
well as wise questions to their satisfaction, the
preacher sought to reduce them to the logical consequences of embracing and teaching the new
religion; but fear of public opinion and motives of
self-interest prevailed against him, and he acknow-
ledges after more than a year that but one
of the priests of Brahm had become a sincere
Christian.

The high-caste Hindoo, acute and apathetic, capable at once of lofty thought and basest practice,
admitting everything, adhering to nothing, professing
in secret a rational faith, teaching in public an imbecile
superstition, was, to a man in whose own life action
had ever followed conviction, a painful problem, a
peculiar trial of patience. With bitter emphasis the
need of this virtue is urged in a series of letters
written to Francis Mancias, who was engaged in
revisiting the villages of the coast, whilst Xavier
himself took charge of the central stations.

In the first he says: "Pray heaven to fortify
your soul with mighty patience, the thing above all

others necessary in dealing with this people. It were
well indeed to consider yourself as being in purgatory
suffering the punishment of your sins, and thank
God that you are granted in this life a season of
expiation."

Again he writes : " I beseech you, dear brother,
with earnest importunity, to treat these perverse
people as a good parent does ungrateful children.
Let not your patience give way before their repeated transgressions and backslidings. The great
God, whom they continually offend, spares them,
when, by a single gesture, he might exterminate
them utterly. He wearies not of providing for all
their wants. Should He withhold His bountiful
hand they would lack all things, and perish miser-
ably even as they have deserved.

" Believe me, your labours in these parts are more
fruitful than you can tell, and though you are not
permitted to see all the results you desire, be well
assured that you are doing good service, such as
needs not to be repented of. However small the
success, you have a sure consolation in the consciousness that you have not remained in idleness,
and have not yourself to blame for the untowardness
of events."

He exhorts him never to fail in gentleness and charity towards the natives, " from the lords and great ones to the lowest of the people, so you will naturally become an object of universal regard among them, your way will be made smooth to you, you will prosper in your ministry on their behalf, and your words will have weight to bring them more readily to the faith and service of the Lord. Show forbearance to all their errors and frailties, with the thought that if they be not virtuous now, they may yet become so ; though it come to pass that you never raise them to the high standard of your hopes, repent not of your efforts, but take comfort in whatever good you may have wrought in them. I also have to console myself in like manner."

In truth, the good Father appears to have found his position a difficult one at this time. The only man of note in a great district half conquered and wholly misgoverned by the Portuguese, he was subject to constant appeals from the oppressed inhabitants, who could not understand that his power to protect them was less than his desire, or that one who had come so far to teach them piety and humanity, should be unable to enforce the same among his own countrymen.

Clear sighted and tender hearted, he perceived from his central vantage-ground a thousand evils of which those at home were ignorant or careless, yet he had no means of influencing the Government, but by the uncertain and tardy course of letters and messengers. All his grievances are poured out to the loyal Mancias with an entire unreserve that seems to admit us to his very heart.

It is impossible not to admire the spirit in which he relates the wrongs whereof three noble Indians, followers of the King of Travancore, came to make complaint to him :

"One of our countrymen, they tell me, has carried off from Patani a servant of the Prince Iniquitribirrimus, has taken him in bonds to Punicale, and has even been heard to boast that he will drag him on with him to Tutucurin. When you shall have learned the truth of this story, write it, I pray you, to the Governor, and if this Portuguese, no matter who he be, can anywhere be found, use all your efforts to make him instantly deliver up his prisoner. Should he be to blame towards the Portuguese, let the case be laid before the Prince, who will give a just decision, and maintain, as he has ever done, the rights of our people. But this advice comes late ; it is the way the thing ought at first to have been done. The subject of an allied sovereign must not be seized, unauthorised by him, within his very dominions, under whatsoever pretext. My distress at the whole affair is greater than words can declare to you. God help us, for it needs strength of mind to withstand patiently disorders and excesses of this nature. I would have you write me (though I have the whole story from credible witnesses) a full and exact account of the circumstances as they come to your own knowledge. Is it a fact that a Portuguese has taken a slave of the King of Travancore, by force, from his own country, and what reason does he assign for the aggression ? Has he really, as I am warned, determined to carry him prisoner to Tutucurin, and with what object ? I would fain discover some circumstances that might mitigate the odium of the crime, and contradict the exaggerations of public rumour ; for, if nothing of the sort appears, and the event has indeed happened as I hear it stated, I must forego my purpose of presenting myself in person before the great king, with whom I had to treat of many things pertaining to God's service.

" Knowing the jealousy with which these people

regard any interference with their slaves, or infrac-
tion of their territory, I cannot doubt that they are
all at this moment meditating bloody vengeance upon
the Portuguese nation, and the Christian name. It
would be bold indeed to go to offer myself a victim
to their wrath.

" I shall be constrained after all to turn my thoughts
to another quarter, to pursue a scheme which has
long possessed great attractions for me ; to abandon
the Indies, where so many obstacles to the propagation of the faith arise in places whence we had least
right to expect them, and to cross over to Ethiopia,
whither we are called by a well-grounded hope of
setting forth the marvellous glory of God, and
spreading the Gospel far and wide in lands where
there will be no Europeans to oppose our teachings,
and overthrow all that we may have achieved. I
will not conceal from you that I am strongly minded
to this course, and may even take passage hence in
one of the native boats, so as to proceed without
delay to Goa, and prepare for my departure to the
dominions of Prester John."

This chapter of the great missionary's life cannot
be more fitly closed than in his own words of advice

and encouragement contained and reiterated in every
letter of the twenty-six received by Mancias during
the year.

" Be not weary in well doing," he says, " never lose
courage, never slacken your endeavours in the slow
and laborious duties of a gospel messenger amidst the
ignorant population of this land.   Visit assiduously
every village, preaching daily to all who will hear
and be careful never to leave in any place the
newly-born infants without baptismal regeneration.
I would fain think that at least the souls which
emigrate early from these little bodies, go to people
that paradise which the elders will not be persuaded
to enter, either by the terror of future punishment, or
the hope of eternal felicity.   Devote your unceasing
attention to secure the religious instruction of the
children, in daily schools ; watching well that the
masters appointed do their teaching thoroughly.
Take care also that the fees of these latter be paid
regularly from the funds at your disposal, and do
not imagine that money or time can ever be better
bestowed, or that you can by any means more
acceptably serve the Lord, than in forwarding the
improvement of the young.   It gives me unspeak-

able satisfaction to learn that you prosper in your
mission, that heavenly consolations are, so to speak,
poured down upon your soul. If God indeed deign
thus to remember you, have a care never to forget
Him. Beware of despondency compromising your
task, nor let the zeal and constancy that you have
hitherto displayed fail you in the end. Keep your
spirit humbled before God in continual thankfulness,
rejoicing always that He has chosen you, and
condescended to use you for so excellent a ministry :
and, lest you be unduly exalted by success, I would
bid you reflect frequently in your own heart, that,
if the mill have ground good meal, the praise thereof
returns to the Supreme Artificer, Master of the
world, who has made the stream to flow that first
turns the wheel and imparts motion and power to
the whole . . . . .

"Again, and yet again, I entreat you not to give
way to any movement of irritation against the
ignorance and weakness of those around you. I
know how trying it is to be disturbed in occupations
of absorbing interest, by persons who insist upon
all your attention for affairs entirely their own.
You must learn, as it were, to govern importunity,
to preserve your own peace of mind, whilst yielding

readily to the various calls upon your time, so as
to perform all that is given you to do, and neglect
only, or defer with perfect equanimity, that which
is, at present, beyond your power . . . . .

"You must try to satisfy, with courteous words,
those whom you are unable to serve, excusing
yourself with a good grace, to prove that you have
at least the will to help them, and consoling them,
wherever it is possible, with some distant hope in
place of the unattainable reality. If you cannot do
all you desire, content yourself with desiring to
do all you can, so long as it does not depend upon
yourself to accomplish everything. When the
claims upon you seem so many as to surpass human
strength, you have but to do your best and rest
satisfied therewith, acknowledging the beneficent
discipline of the Providence that has set you in a
place where idleness at least is impossible, and where
you have no leisure to listen to temptation . . . . .

" Take heed to the preservation of your health ;
it is an indispensable instrument for the service
in which you have already displayed so much
activity . . . . .

"It seems to me that I have not sufficiently
enjoined upon you the importance of making, with

unalterable perseverance and zeal, a continual round of the villages throughout the country. Do not take up your abode in any place, nor delay long in visiting each one of the churches to preach the word of God and administer the sacraments wherever there are Christians in need of them. I recommend to you, equally with the laymen, the priests and clerks lately ordained from among the natives of Malabar. Watch over their way of life, give them wise and friendly counsel, and use such means as circumstances admit to guide them in piety and chastity, that they exercise their vocation to the glory of God and show their countrymen a good example of innocence and virtue. Be courteous to all men, especially the magistrates, and deal tenderly with the aged, gaining love and respect wherever you go. If sometimes the malice of mankind seems to render your gentleness of none effect, I would have you use a certain severity, for it is also a work of mercy to chastise criminals, above all when their impunity causes scandal to others. Nevertheless I do not think that at such critical moments, nor indeed at any other time, we should abandon the sinner to his fate. I pity far too much the misfortune of such as are separated from their Heavenly Father to wish to call down upon them the Divine wrath. Can we doubt that God will at last avenge Himself on His foes with terrible punishment, even that of hell and death eternal."

We find the same rules of conduct laid down at greater length and with more precision and formality in a letter of instruction, addressed at a later date, to the missionaries in Travancore. Next after the baptism and education of the younger generation, they are charged to devote their care to the healing of feuds and the amendment of morals. They are desired to base their teaching upon the Ten Commandments, to disseminate everywhere copies of the articles of faith and their explanation in the Malabar tongue, and "to have them publicly read every Sunday with a clear, loud and intelligible voice," preaching afterwards upon the wonderful judgments of God, and the necessity of repentance and godly life. They are recommended to use persuasion and gentleness, seeking to be loved rather than feared ; to make personal sacrifices in order to keep on good terms with their countrymen, but to be bold in defending the natives from their injustice and contempt ; to act as peacemakers in private, but to avoid interference in disputes and lawsuits upon temporal affairs, which encroach upon the time, weaken the authority and lower the high calling of God's priests. They are cautioned, also, to be scrupulously honest and exact in the application of moneys entrusted to them for the building of churches and the support of schools, to hand over at once to the poor any sums received in payment of vows or thank-offerings, nor ever consent to accept the smallest portion for their personal use. Finally, they are to be faithful in rendering account of their works, submissive to authorities, temporal and spiritual, and not lightly tempted to forsake their appointed place, even at the solicitation of kings and princes.

CHAPTER IX

TROUBLE

'' Guide our barque among the waves,
   Through the rocks our passage smooth
  When the whirlpool frets and raves.
   Let thy love its anger soothe,
    All our hope is placed in Thee
   Miserere Domine.''

                      WORDSWORTH.

FROM the time of his first arrival in India, Xavier had cherished the hope that, after providing for the spiritual wants of the scattered tribes at the fishery, he would be enabled to push on to the thickly populated provinces beyond, and obtain audience of some of the ruling princes who, once converted to the true faith, must greatly help his efforts for the benefit of their subjects. Thus the new religion, spreading from an accredited centre, might make sure and rapid progress, and Christianity be planted

in the heart of the country instead of merely grafted
on the outermost branches of the great Hindoo race.
The kingdom of Travancore extended at this time
over a great part of Southern India, and to its
monarch, styled (probably by translation of the
name into monks' Latin) Iniquitribirrimus, he long
sought to address himself, trusting to obtain at
least protection for the Christians against the hosts
of irregular soldiery called Badages, who continually
harassed the frontier. More than once he had been
promised an interview with this potentate, and
prevented by some gross breach of faith, on the part
of his countrymen, from availing himself of the much
desired opening. Can we wonder that such vexa-
tious hindrances drew from him wild hints of a
visit to Prester John (who he believed to be in Abys-
sinia) and despairing assertions, that it were better
to die a martyr than to live and witness such sinful
resistance to the progress of truth. " Often I
weary of existence," he cries, "when I can neither
control these things or cease from beholding
them."

We learn in a later letter to Mancias that Francis
persevered against all obstacles in negotiations with
his royal neighbour:

"Dear Brother in the Lord,—

"An intense longing to see you once more possesses me, and I trust that God in His mercy will soon satisfy my desire. In the meantime no day passes but I am with you in spirit, and I doubt not your heart is with me also, so we are in truth never parted from each other. I beseech you, for the love of God, write to me about yourself, about all the Christians, about your health, your affairs and all that concerns you. I would fain hear everything minutely and precisely.

"I am expecting here this week one of the lords of Travancore; he will not surely fail to come, having himself been at the pains of writing to apprise me of his arrival. What more can I tell you, but that my heart is overflowing with confident hopes of the good that my be effected at this meeting. Whatever takes place, you shall learn from us speedily, that you may give thanks to God.

"Both the Father who is with me, and I myself, are in excellent health.

"Tell the boy Matthew, from me, to continue in good behaviour, and to be careful to pronounce the lessons you have taught him, loudly and very clearly, at the catechism meetings. When I come, I

will bring him some little present, which I doubt not
will give him pleasure.

" Do the children still come willingly to repeat the
prayers at the appointed times, and do many of them
possess the gift of memory ?   Spare, I pray you,
neither words nor paper in giving me a full account
of your works, and send me letters by the very first
person bound hitherwards.   The Lord be with you,
as I trust He will be with me also.   Farewell.

" LIVARES, *April* 23, 1544."

Still awaiting the royal messenger, Francis was
laid low for many days with jungle fever.   Weak-
ened and dispirited, he worked his way back to
Manapore, ·his headquarters at the midmost point
of the great bay of Manaar.   There the news of
a terrible calamity roused him speedily to his wonted
vigour for a work of practical charity.   The Christians of Cape Comorin, he heard, had been attacked,
overcome, and scattered by the Badages, and the
greater part led away captive.   The rest, taking
refuge in the caverns and rocky islets of the sea,
were perishing of hunger and thirst.   His prompt
measures for the relief of these latter are thus
recorded by his own pen.

"I had set forth with twenty boats laden with provisions, to succour the Christians who have fled before the Badages to the utmost rocks of Comorin, and lie there a prey to mortal anguish, and drought, and famine, but contrary winds raging violently, we were able neither with helm nor oars to make head against the current, nor to land so much as one of our barques. If the storm cease, I shall again embark for that destination, to bear what relief is in my power to these unfortunates in their extreme distress. It would be cruel indeed to slacken or cease in our endeavours to remedy a misfortune, the greatest in the world, that has befallen these wretched people, worshippers of the Lord, even as we ourselves. Every day, numbers of them come to seek shelter at Manapore, naked and emaciated by famine, despoiled of all things. I am writing to the Patangats of Coimbatour, Punicale and Tutucurin, bidding them collect alms for the sufferers, exacting nothing from the poor, neither constraining the rich, but exhorting them to send us according to the measure of their charity. I wish, indeed I think it necessary, that you (Francis Mancias) bestir yourself in the matter, as the justice and wisdom of the magistrates inspire .me with little confidence.

"Heaven only knows what I have suffered in this expedition, having been eight days at sea. You can imagine, from your own experience, the discomfort of being on board these little boats in such a gale as we have had, so strong that no human arms nor exertions could prevail against it."

At last, he tells us, he succeeded in reaching by land the victims of the Badages' (or brigand) incursion. "Never has any one beheld a more horrible scene. Faces pallid and distorted by hunger; here the scorched ground strewn with corpses, unburied and loathsome, there men expiring beneath the burning sun from untended wounds and maladies without cure. Old men, bowed down with years and privation, trying vainly to totter onward; women become mothers in their flight, sinking, for want of sustenance, before their husband's eyes. I have taken care to transport the most wretched to Manapore, where, indeed, a great part of this distressed population are already to be found, with whom we have to deal according to our means. Pray the Lord that He may speak to the hearts of the rich, and inspire them with compassion for the many miserable ones who are perishing here in utter desolation."

A month later the inhabitants of Tutucurin were overtaken by a like disastrous fate, and Mancias is despatched to the rescue by the following missive :

" Grievous news has reached me concerning the Governor of Tutucurin. His fleet has been burned, his houses and possessions destroyed by fire. Without resources, having lost his all, he has fled to the isles, where he still preserves a miserable existence. Hasten to help him for holy charity's sake, with all the vessels you can find at Punicale, taking abundant provisions ; and, above all things, a supply of good water, in which these isles are sadly deficient. Speed your best, for his state of absolute destitution admits of no delay, and see that there be boats enough to bring back to the mainland the crowd of fugitives driven by the same blow to those inhospitable rocks. I would go myself, leaving you in peace at Punicale, could I hope that my presence would be acceptable ; but this man has, not long ago, declared me his enemy in a letter full of violent accusations. God and men know whether I have done him wrong. However, this is not the time to justify my actions, or complain of his, only, knowing his feelings towards me, you will understand that I

avoid meeting him for his own sake. My presence
would be galling to him in his humiliation, and the
sight of my face would add bitterness to his woe. I
am exhorting the Patangats of Coimbatour and
Bembar to collect instantly all the boats at their
disposal, and speed them with water and provisions
to the place, and you, as you would do the service of
our heavenly Master, put forth your utmost zeal in
the matter, that you may never have to regret that
you failed in timely succour to one fallen suddenly
from high estate.

" We owe him every good office of kindness and
pity, and our charity must extend to all the Christian
sufferers wrecked, as it were, in the same tempest, of
whom the bare thought makes me beseech you to
neglect nothing that may bring them swift and effec-
tual aid in their dire extremity."

To provide against the recurrence of such calamities
was the province of the civil rather than the religious
authorities, but the whole district had now become a
scene of confusion and terror, and there was no one
there capable of organising resistance or obtaining
redress. The missionaries stood alone amidst a
timid and helpless population, whose docility in

accepting the Gospel had brought upon them the vengeance of evil and bloodthirsty men. Father Francis at once took the head of affairs, writing to Mancias as follows :

" Nothing on earth could tempt me to forsake these people in their hour of danger and tribulation, neither would I have you persuaded to depart with Joam d'Artiaga, at least until these troubles be past. It grieves me beyond measure to think that your presentiment of being taken prisoner may perhaps be some day realised ; but in truth I share all your alarm on that score. Only, if so great a misfortune should happen to you, be very sure that I shall never rest until God restore you to us—I trust speedily. I also, believe me, am encompassed with the like perils and anxieties ; nevertheless, let all be done to the glory of the good God, our sovereign Lord.

" I have despatched one of our priests along the coast with notice to the villages that they equip and launch their boats, to be ready for instant embarkation and flight when the brigands invade the country, which I hear they are now preparing to do, in great force. My informant is one of the great chiefs, very favourable to the native Christians. I had sent him a letter, addressed to the King of Travancore, praying him to deliver it in person, since he is much esteemed by that Prince, and to use all his influence and earnest solicitations to support my petition, and persuade his Sovereign to put down, with royal authority, all future incursions upon the territory of our unhappy converts. I added, that the Viceroy of the Indies would consider their injuries his own, and avenge them accordingly.

"I had good reason to trust that this chief would do something on our behalf, being a friend of mine, and, as I told you before, well disposed towards the Christians, among whom are many of his own relations. He came to me himself, not merely to show respect, but to proffer help and service on this occasion. Now I had written to him that, if it were not possible to put an immediate check on the depredations of the Badages, he should at least give me timely warning of their movements, thus we might arrange beforehand for the embarkation of our people, and send them and theirs fairly to sea beyond reach of spoliation and massacre. This warning he has now faithfully given.

"I have written also to the Viceroy beseeching him to send one of his armed vessels for the protection of all these defenceless boats. Never cease exhorting the inhabitants, especially such as live away from the shore, to establish a watch at every commanding point, that they may be roused in time, not surprised by some midnight raid of cavalry and cut off before they can reach the boats. But having done all this, I would not advise you to trust much to the effect of your words. I know too well the indolence and provoking obstinacy of these folks ; they will grudge the expense of the necessary sentinels. Watch them and act for yourself ; make your own followers launch their barques immediately, and see that the women and children are put on board the first. Do not fail either to improve this season of trial, by impressing upon all, especially such as are most helpless by age and sex, the needs of making supplication to God. Fear is a great teacher of prayer, above all when, as with these poor souls, there is no hope but in God alone.

" My store of writing paper is exhausted, but I left with you a quantity in a box, which I will beg you to send me as soon as possible. By the same messenger I shall expect to hear from you that the embarkation is progressing, that the little property of the families exposed to danger, and their household goods are being placed in safety, as well as the mothers and children. If this has not yet been done, you must bestir yourself in the matter. Go at once to Antonio Fernandez, and entreat him, by his friendship for me, to assist these unfortunate people, to use his authority in forwarding their preparations, to make them perceive that not their liberty only is at stake, but their lives—yea, their flesh and blood; for, while the rich among them may perchance be carried off in hope of ransom, the poor, from whom avarice can expect nothing, will be sacrificed by these bloodthirsty robbers. Again, first and foremost, I counsel you to lose no time in appointing watchers all along the coast, at least during these nights when the full moon may light the enemy's march.

"God have you in His keeping, for He only is infallible. Farewell.

"Your loving brother in the Lord,

"FRANCIS."

Badages, according to the early biographers, were—"Barbarians by nature, Gentiles in religion, and robbers by profession;" in fact, direct emissaries of the evil one, and, as such, we hear that they were speedily put to rout by the mere presence of the holy man, who is said to have scattered a whole army of them, by advancing at the head of a few trembling converts, "with uplifted cross and sonorous rebuke, in a language unknown and terrible, with awful eyes in a face of unearthly pallor, flashing from beneath his sable cowl. A moment they stood spell-bound, watching their flight of arrows fall harmlessly around their opponent, then they turned and fled away, no man pursuing."

Meanwhile, by patient negotiations, threats of Portuguese interference, appeals to patriotic, commercial, and even personal motives, the good Father did at length succeed in securing some shadow of peace for his afflicted pearl-divers. Not until he had seen them restored to their homes or established in new ones, and unmolested in the pursuit of their perilous calling; until he had himself relieved their wants, visited their sick, baptized their new-born babes, reassembled the children's classes and the weekly meetings for public worship; not, in fact, until he had replaced the church at Comorin in working order, did he permit himself to proceed on any further mission. His presentation

to the King of Travancore, accomplished this time
in spite of all difficulties, does not seem to have
afforded any grounds on which to build up fresh
hopes. No record of the actual interview is left us
in the letters (the writer having probably found
opportunity to visit his correspondent on his return
and relate his adventures in person), but we gather,
by degrees, that the temporary suppression of the
Badages, and toleration of the new faith, were its
main results. The monarch appears to have been
gracious only from political considerations (re-
quiring Portuguese assistance against his too
powerful lords, &c.), and would not, by any means,
be persuaded himself to become a Christian. Among
his subjects, however, many converts were made,
and churches and schools established, at the royal
expense, by priests from the Fishery still acting
under Xavier's directions.

CHAPTER X

WANDERINGS

" Seize the banner, spread its fold,
Seize it with no faltering hold,
Spread its foldings high and fair ;
Let all see the Cross is there.

" What if to the trumpet sound
Voices few come answering round,
God will aid the work begun,
For the love of His dear Son."

KEBLE.

THE Indies of the sixteenth century lay mainly to the south of the Peninsula of Hindostan, the interior of which had hardly been explored by the Portuguese, while their utmost settlements extended no farther on the north-eastern coast than St. Thomas of Miliapur, now lying in ruin close to the modern city of Madras. The innumerable islands with their rich products and convenient ports, and various advantages of climate and population, were of far

more importance in European eyes than the continent itself; and Xavier must have heard many
marvellous accounts of them and their inhabitants
during the two years that he had been journeying
to and fro upon the coast opposite Ceylon. Indeed,
he and Mancias had already paid some short visit
to that land of Eden, appropriated by tradition as
the scene of our first parents' abode, but seemingly
now delivered over to the angels of darkness in the
shape of petty tyrants, cruel, sensual, and wilfully
ignorant. In spite of this malignant influence, a
few brave men had already succeeded in planting
the cross at the foot of Adam's Peak, and preaching
its mercies to the long-suffering Cingalese. Their
words were listened to, even in the King's palace,
and the heir to the throne professed himself a
convert. He was immediately put to death by
command of his father, and his body cast out to be
devoured by the wild beasts and the fowls of heaven.
Men said that the ground where it lay opened in
the form of a cross to give him Christian burial,
and Francis relates that infinite numbers were
thereby moved to become Christians. Francis, probably in his capacity of inspector of missions to His
Portuguese Majesty, returned to the continent with

H

a brother of the murdered prince, who had desired admission into the same faith and was forced into exile in consequence.

He tells us that he held many interesting conversations with the royal fugitive by the way, and desired exceedingly to see the intelligent God-fearing youth succeed to the throne, and rule, as he confidently hoped, over an entirely Christian people. He did not, however, feel justified in prompting the Government to active interference on this occasion as in the more aggravated case of the persecution of the Christians of Manaar by the neighbouring King of Jafnapatan, who reigned in the extreme north of the island. That affair, which was the immediate cause of his leaving the Comorin coast, is thus related in his own words :

"The inhabitants of Manaar, an island some hundred and fifty miles distant, sent me messengers, beseeching me to come and baptize them, since they were resolved to make themselves Christians. I could not immediately yield to their request, being detained by other matters of grave import to the cause of religion, but I sought out a venerable priest, willing to go in my stead so soon as the thing was possible, and regenerate them by the waters of baptism. Through his cares very many had received the sacred rite, when the King of Jafnapatan, suzerain of the island, caused the whole congregation of converts to be put to a cruel death, only because they had professed themselves Christians.

"Blessed be the Lord Jesus, who has suffered these things to be done even in our own times—who has permitted, in the mystery of His Providence, that the few who bear witness in their lives to the divine goodness and mercy, shall be strengthened by the host of martyrs passing through death unto salvation; so that human barbarity is left, as it were, to fill up the ranks and complete the reckoning of the redeemed."

Xavier's remarks on this subject were more patient and philosophic than his actions; for, leaving to his assistants the charge of his new converts in Travancore, he hastened through that country to Cochin, and thence to Cambay, to plead in person with the Viceroy for the immediate chastisement of the offending monarch. "I have told you very often," he continues to his European brethren, "how well disposed the Governor of all the Indies has shown himself to support me and our Company in all things. Moreover, he was so moved with horror on learning of the bloody slaughter of the neophytes, that he had commanded the arming of a great fleet for the extermination of the tyrant almost before I had opened my mouth on the matter; and I have rather to restrain than excite the vehemence of his just indignation. Now the lawful heir to the throne of this royal executioner is a brother, whom the terror of his cruelties has driven into exile. This prince has promised for himself and all his followers to accept Christianity, if put in possession of his just inheritance. So the Viceroy has ordered the Portuguese captains to place him on the throne upon these conditions, and to put the oppressor to death, or leave him to be dealt with according to my will. I do not utterly despair that the mercy of God and the prayers of those martyred ones may, even yet, bring him to the consciousness of his great crime; and that, by wholesome penitence, he may at last obtain God's pardon for his atrocious barbarity."

Xavier had another object in returning at this

time to the haunts of civilisation ; to confer with
Miguel Vaz, the Vicar-General, before his departure
for Portugal, and entrust him with letters and
statements of importance to lay before the home
Government. These two men, the most earnest,
and in some respects the most enlightened, in all
India, met at Cochin, in December 1544, and spent
many days and weeks together, making arrange-
ments for the welfare of the churches they had
founded, and discussing, in the refreshment of mutual
confidence, matters that lay very near the hearts
of both.

"You will hardly find anywhere," Xavier writes
to his old colleague, Simon Rodriguez, "a man so
filled with zeal and devotion to the service and
glory of God, as Miguel Vaz. I cannot doubt that
his presence and discourse will be most welcome to
you, for, only in beholding the peace and serenity
that shine on his countenance, you will not fail to
form an exalted notion and a most just estimate of his
worth. You may entirely trust his every word, and
he will place before you, in full and without reserve,
the present state of our affairs in the Indies."

At the same date he writes to the King of
Portugal, as follows :

" Sire,

" If it be indeed permitted me to point out to
your Majesty the sentiments by which I would have
you actuated, let me bid you look into yourself, and
consider how Our Lord has chosen you out before
all other princes of the earth, and bestowed upon
you this great empire of the Indies, to try and to
prove your virtue, your faithfulness in a Sovereign's
duties, and your gratitude for infinite benefits. The
design of Providence was not to fill your treasury
with the precious products of the East, and the
gold of barbarian kings ; but to give scope to your
heroism, to afford your piety and benevolence new
opportunities of development, and to prepare, by
your ardent zeal, a way whereby the efforts of your
faithful servants may avail to bring the inhabitants
of these regions to the knowledge of the Creator
and Saviour of the world.

" Your Majesty, then, may well make it the first
duty of your envoys in the East to extend the rule
of Christianity on every side, and propagate our
holy faith ; conscious that God will demand from
you a reckoning of all these your people, who are
ready to enter into the way of truth if any man
would direct them therein, whom the want of

teachers leaves in the darkness of ignorance and
the depths of degradation, where they incessantly
offend their Maker, and fit their souls for eternal
ruin and damnation.

"From the report of Dom Miguel Vaz, coadjutor
to the Bishop of Goa, now returning to Portugal,
your Majesty will learn the disposition that prevails
among the natives to embrace our faith, and other
circumstances favourable to the progress of religion,
whereof he himself can bear witness. He leaves
behind him such deep regret in the hearts of all the
Christians in the land, that his return seems almost
a necessity for their consolation and spiritual well-
being. Your Majesty will indeed serve your own
highest interests in sending back to Goa forthwith a
minister as wise as he is zealous in the business he
has undertaken—the promotion of the knowledge and
glory of God throughout the Indies. Having charged
this faithful and experienced servant with the
execution of your wishes, your soul may be at rest,
assured that the rare merits which have won the
veneration of a whole people will be an earnest of
his vigilance, in losing no opportunity of supporting
and forwarding the cause of religion. The Bishop,
no doubt, is a prelate of consummate virtue, but your

Majesty must be aware that advanced age and numerous infirmities have deprived him of the physical strength needful for the immense labours of his charge. He has preserved only the powers of his mind, which become truly ever more admirable ; the weakness of his body being overcome by the fulness of spiritual grace. Even thus the Lord recompenses His faithful ones after a lifelong devotion to His service, after the sacrifice of time and strength to great works undertaken for His sake. It is the triumph of the spirit over the flesh, the crown that divine goodness permits a few valiant athletes to grasp in their declining days, for the example and encouragement of those who follow after and see them born again, as it were, by a renewal of the mental forces, when nature, failing and enfeebled, is already verging upon dissolution. As life passes away from these venerable mortals, their earthly body is gradually transfigured into a heavenly spirit. Surely now, more than ever, our saintly Bishop has need of some vigorous helper in the arduous duties of his Apostolate.

"Call to remembrance, Sire, your former ardour, the delicacy of conscience with which you were wont to acquit yourself of every obligation of your high position, as in the sight of God alone ; I adjure you thus for the safety of your own soul. Send to the Indies a Governor, armed with the necessary powers to protect and provide for the infinity of human souls that stand imperilled at this hour. Above all things, let his authority be independent of that of the Crown treasures, that the malversations and scandals which have disgraced Christendom be avoided henceforth.

"In charity I write thus to your Majesty, in the compassion that burns for you in the depths of my heart, when I seem to hear accusing voices rising up to Heaven to complain that our King has acted the niggard towards this empire, grudging, out of all the treasure with which it has enriched him, a small portion to provide for its people's greatest and abiding want. Send us, gracious Sovereign, yet many of the working brethren of our order, that they may not only be sufficient to baptize the crowds that come forward daily in these parts, to join our religion, but may also be sent to Malacca and the neighbouring States, where frequent conversions are even now taking place.

"Francis Mancias bears me company upon the

Comorin coast, among the Christians first converted by Dom Miguel Vaz. With us also are three native priests.

"That I shall die in the Indies and see your face no more on earth, is to me a perfect certainty: therefore I do entreat the aid of your prayers that we may meet again in the blessed abode of peace. Supplicate for me, as I shall for your Majesty, that we may so think and act in every circumstance of life, as we shall desire to have done, when we draw near the hour of death.

"Your Majesty's servant,

"FRANCIS."

" COCHIN, *Feb. 8th*, 1545."

Whether in consequence of this letter or no, the Governor De Soza was recalled and to his successor the King writes as follows :

"The first obligation of a Christian ruler is to watch over the interests of religion and maintain the faith by all means in his power. The same causes me to communicate to you that I have learned with deep sorrow that, not only in many parts of our Indian dominions, but in our own city of Goa, and places where Christianity ought assuredly to flourish, false gods are still objects of public worship.

"Now, being fully aware that heathen ceremonies are performed in the light of day, we command you to search out the idols and destroy them, and break them in pieces wheresoever they be found, and to publish rigorous penalties against any person who shall dare henceforth to make, mould, grave, design or paint, produce or import, any idolatrous image in metal or bronze, wood, clay, or any other substance, &c.

"We have been informed, to our great grief, by reverend men worthy of all credence, that certain Portuguese are in the practice of buying slaves at a low price, to dispose of them afterwards to the Moors and other unbelieving traders for the sake of iniquitous profits. Thus they damage even the souls of these unhappy creatures, who might otherwise be converted to our faith. Use your best endeavours to check this evil, to put a stop to this traffic. You will perform a service pleasing to God, and very satisfactory to us, if by the exercise of due severity you can restrain so serious an abuse.

"In all cases and upon every point we desire you to hold counsel with Father Francis Xavier. Examine with him more especially whether it be really conducive to the influence of religion on the Fishery stations to let the new converts dwell in idleness. If you decide upon permitting them so to do, it should be well seen that, with their new creed, they have put on new morals and put away the licence of their former lives. We are warned, on the other hand, that many who have forsworn paganism for our pure faith, find themselves despised and maltreated by their relations and neighbours, who hunt them from their dwellings, and despoil them of their goods, so that they are often reduced to extreme penury and hardly sustain life by weary and unceasing toil. You will do well to employ the Vicar Miguel Vaz to relieve the misery of these, entrusting him with funds from our treasury, to be distributed by the priest, according to his best judgment.

"A young man from Ceylon, we have been advised, has lately taken refuge at Goa, to escape the rage and fury of his near relations. He is reputed to be of royal blood, with rights of succession to the throne of his country. Now it seems good to us, in consideration of his profession of Christianity, and for the encouragement of other neophytes, that he should be worthily received at

the College of St. Paul in that town. Entertain him,
therefore, at our cost suitably to his high birth, that
our liberal intentions towards persons of the like noble
character may be seen of all men. At the same
time, take pains to inquire closely into the reality
of his pretensions, and forward to us the result of
your investigations, that we may take such measures
as are desirable. It is our will that you forthwith
bring the tyrant of Ceylon to strict account for the
barbarous treatment he has seen fit to inflict upon
his subjects newly converted to our holy faith.
Oblige him to give such satisfaction for these acts of
detestable cruelty, that all the rulers of India may
acknowledge that justice is dear to us, and that we
are ever ready to protect the oppressed."

During the two years that these affairs were
pending, Father Francis pursued a somewhat de-
sultory course of voyages from port to port, guided
at times by inspired dreams, driven at times by the
force of outward circumstances, at the mercy often
of the winds and waves ; but ever intent upon one
object, ever busied in clearing a way for Gospel
truth to the hearts of benighted lands, and of ignorant
and misguided men. About Jafnapatan we quote

his own words :—"This expedition has ended in naught I The prince who promised to become a Christian has not been reinstated in his inheritance. An evil chance has ruined all. A ship that belonged to the King of Portugal, returning from Pegu with a rich cargo, was caught by the tempest and driven ashore upon the coast of Jafnapatan. The king of the country seized the merchandize, and the Portuguese have thought it expedient to hush up the war until restitution of their property be secured. So the Viceroy's orders have not been regarded, but they shall yet be fulfilled, if it please God."

These sudden changes of policy threw Francis into great perplexity and indecision of mind with regard to his own further movements. "Oh, that Our Lord," he exclaims, "would grant us the grace so ardently desired, so long awaited—the grace to know by some sure sign His holy will—where He would have me to go ?—how but to proclaim His glory ? We hold ourselves in readiness to obey the first call, to fulfil instantly the divine behests, be the difficulties never so great. Marvellous indeed are the ways whereby the Lord makes manifest His intent. A secret conviction penetrates the soul and illumines its darkest depths, as with a ray from

Heaven. To those in whom this light is revealed, there remains no more uncertainty concerning the ways or the works destined for them by Providence. It has been said, and with perfect truth, that mortals passing over the face of the earth must needs, by law and condition of their nature, acknowledge themselves as strangers and travellers here below, nor suffer themselves to be withheld by attachment to any place or object from a free flight whither-soever their reason points to the highest good, the aim and end of their hopes and their existence. So ought we ourselves ever to stand ready for a summons to regions and employments the most foreign, and oftentimes the most distasteful to our minds. Our ardour must prepare us to accept all things with great alacrity, and speed at the bidding of our Heavenly Master ; east, west, south or north, all alike in our eyes, and our choice determined solely by the greater or less results which each enterprise promises for the honour and glory of God."

His final resolution and the manner of its adoption were communicated to the Fathers at Goa in some-what more guarded terms. "I remained for many days at Myapatan, till at last the winds, adverse to my return, changed the direction of my voyage.

Suffering myself to be led by circumstances, I came to the town of St. Thomas. In the venerable sanctuary of the Apostle, I failed not to beseech the Lord with fervent supplication that He would deign to discover to me His will, since I was resolved to follow it entirely. I trusted that He who gives us to will any good thing shall give likewise the power to do it. In His infinite mercy the Lord remembered His servant. With a thrill of joy, that penetrated my inmost soul, I perceived that I was called of God to Malacca, and thence to Macassar, where many are already turning to Christ, and need to be strengthened in the faith. I have had the elements and precepts of our religion, with short explanations of the same, translated into their language ; for is it not reasonable that those who have joined us of their own free will, should receive at our hands every assistance ? They should have prayers in their own tongue, wherewith to petition for the increase of their faith and strength to keep the commandments of the divine law ; a form of general confession to use daily, for acknowledging their sins before God, in lieu of sacramental confession, so long as they have not among them any priest capable of understanding their speech.

" I trust that God will bestow upon me special protection during this voyage. Of a truth, as I have now told you, He has not disdained to reveal to me His sovereign will, and I am so firmly resolved to fulfil the inspiration of Providence, that should I indeed have the misfortune to fail in this matter, it would seem to me that I had revolted against Heaven, and was cut off from hope, in life, or in death. If it happen that I find within the year no opportunity of making the passage by a Portuguese ship, I shall not hesitate to trust myself in any Saracen or Indian trader bound for Malacca. So unshaken is my confidence in Him for whose sake alone I undertake this voyage, that even though there sail not any merchant vessel at all this year, but only the most miserable boat for my destination, I shall still embark without fear, assured that divine help is ever at hand.

" As I have put my trust in God alone, I entreat you, beloved brethren, to commend me to Him, me a miserable sinner, in your holy Masses every day, and in your continual prayers. Towards the end of August I think to depart, since it is about that time that the favourable winds most commonly arise."

I

CHAPTER XI

THE INDIAN ARCHIPELAGO

" As o'er each continent and island
The dawn leads on another day,
The voice of prayer is never silent,
Nor dies the strain of praise away."

HYMNS A. & M.

" Lone on the land, and homeless on the water,
Pass I in patience till the work be done.

" Yet not in solitude, if Christ anear me
Waketh Him workers for the great employ.
O not in solitude, if souls that hear me
Catch from my joyaunce the surprise of joy ! "

F. W. MYERS.

EXACTLY six months later (November, 1545), this pioneer of Christianity gives the following account of his further proceedings :

" Since my arrival some weeks ago at Malacca, a very famous port, by reason of the concourse of merchants frequenting it, I have not wanted for spiritual occupation. On Sunday I preach to the assembled inhabitants of the city, who seem in truth better pleased with my exhortations than I myself am content therewith. Every morning I devote an hour or more to teaching the children some simple prayers of our Church. The remainder of the day is spent in the hospital, where I hear the confessions of the sick, celebrate Mass, and administer the Sacrament. My penitents come in so great number that I sometimes know not how to deal with them all. Besides this, I employ much of my time in translating the Catechism from the Latin into the language used in Macassar; it is so painful to be quite ignorant of the speech of those about one.

"Whilst awaiting the ship that should bring me hither, I fell in with a merchant, disembarking his goods at the port of St. Thomas. The man, having some perception of spiritual things, speedily began to comprehend the existence of merchandise more precious than aught of his, albeit hidden until now from his quest. Therefore, forsaking at once his trade and his possessions, he came to proffer me his fellowship, and bear me company likewise in my voyage to Macassar. Jean D'Eyro by name, he is thirty years of age, and a soldier of the world up to this day. He has now resolved to embrace holy poverty for the remainder of his life, and enlist with heart and soul in the service of Jesus Christ ; wherefore he desires the favour of your prayers that he may be accepted of the Lord.

" Letters from Rome as well as from Lisbon have followed me hither. The comfort they have given and still give me is greater than words can tell. Each time I read them over, and that is very often, I can fancy that you are here with me, or that I am in Europe again with you. If it may not be so in the body, then in the spirit.

" I have but one prayer to make to you, my dear brethren ; that there come after us every year many members of our order, for truly there are many needed. Not great literary attainments are required for the conversion of the heathen, but virtue seasoned by long experience."

The latter sentiment is still more strongly expressed in a little note written from this place to Simon Rodriguez at Coimbra, not otherwise interesting to us. Nor is there much worthy of notice in the letter to Paul di Camerino and the newly arrived brethren at Goa. We miss the frank outpourings to Francis Mancias, who seems, one cannot tell how, to have forfeited his place in his leader's confidence. His name is now only mentioned incidentally, the new-comers being recommended to take him as their guide at Comorin ; afterwards he is summoned along with them to Malacca, where, however, he never appears. Thenceforth no word more is heard of him in the letters, those which might have thrown light on the cause of estrangement having been perhaps suppressed by the biographers, who tell us only that he was turned out of the Society for disobedience, by Xavier himself, in 1547; that he persevered nevertheless in good works, and died in great sanctity at Contam some twenty years later.

The great missionary found his scheme of an expedition to Macassar forestalled by a priest sent thither by the authorities at Malacca under escort of a military force. He was urged to wait for the return of the ship that had conveyed these warlike Gospel-bearers, before risking more lives on the faith of flattering rumours already half discredited. He yielded for a time, and began to turn his thoughts to other islands in the neighbourhood, as greatly in need of spiritual enlightenment as Macassar, and in January 1546 set sail once more, in a vessel bound for the Banda Isles, which put him, with his new comrade, John D'Eyro, ashore at Amboyna on the 16th of February in the same year.

" For when," writes he, " I saw that the favourable winds had ceased, and still there came no tidings of the priest and soldiers that had been sent to Macassar, I thought it not right to delay longer, and leaving Malacca, departed forthwith for the Moluccas.

" At the farthest extreme of these islands the King of Portugal holds a fortified place called Sernate. Some two hundred miles thence, but nearer the Indies, is the island of Amboyna, with a great population both of natives and foreigners. It has been bestowed by his Majesty upon a Portuguese lord of illustrious virtue and piety, who comes, they say, in a year or two, to settle here with his wife and children, and all his household. It contains but seven Christian villages, all of which I have visited, baptizing the young children, and many others who had not received the sacred rite. Some of them departed this life but a little while afterwards, so that it seemed that their existence had been prolonged only until the way of eternal life was opened to them.

"About that time eight Spanish vessels put into harbour here for three months. With what diverse occupations I was overwhelmed during their stay! With constant preaching I strove to incite the members of the different crews to a sober and godly life. I heard their confessions, I comforted them in sickness ; I stood by them in the hour of death, that they might quit the world in faith and resignation ; difficult sentiments for men who had long lived in contempt of all the divine laws. Such people dis‑ play, in their last moments, much as terror of death and despair of God's mercy, as they had formerly shown boldness in plunging into the mire of in‑ numerable crimes. Nevertheless, many who had lived in violence and strife, no rare condition among men who have made war their calling, were by especial grace reconciled to their enemies, and restored to lasting peace.

"At last the fleet sailed for the Indies, and I, accompanied by Jean D'Eyro, of whom I have spoken to you, went on in the opposite direction— that is to say, towards the Moluccas.

"Beyond them again, perhaps at two hundred

miles distance, lies the land of Moro (Gilolo), where, long years ago, many of the inhabitants made profession of Christianity ; but, being neglected, left orphans, so to speak, by the death of the priest who had instructed them, have fallen back into ignorance and primitive barbarism. 'Tis a region full of peril to travellers, as the people are savage in the extreme, and are much given to mix poison in the food they offer strangers. The fear of their cruelty has hitherto withheld any priest from extending his ministry to these islanders ; but, beholding the immensity of their wants, with none to teach them any good or to purify them by holy sacraments, I feel myself constrained to strive after their salvation even at the risk of death. I am determined to make my way thither so soon as it be possible, and to face whatever dangers may beset my path. Verily I have put my hope in the Lord, and will, so far as in me lies, prove the words of Jesus : ' Whosoever will save his life, shall lose it ; and whosoever will lose his life for My sake, shall find it.'

"The precept seems very simple to the understanding, but in practice it is far otherwise. When the hour is come to lose one's life to find it again only in Heaven—when the perils of death are imminent and we see clearly that to obey the Lord may cost us our existence—the brightness of the promise is overshadowed, we know not how, and hidden in the great darkness. The wisest men are powerless to comprehend this glorious sentence, which is only realised by those within whose hearts God Himself is a ruling presence through the special gift of His grace. It is on such occasions that the weakness and infirmity of our nature stands revealed in the light of day.

" My friends here conjured me not to venture amongst these savages, and since they could not persuade me, even with tears and prayers, they brought me, every one, some new charm or antidote against poison, but I refused them all, lest the number of the remedies should lay upon me another burden, that of fear, from which I have hitherto been exempt. My trust is in Providence ; I dare not rely upon any human help to distract my thoughts from God ; therefore I thanked them, and besought them only to pray for me—that is the true safeguard after all.

" To look back at our voyage to the Moluccas. It was far from favourable. We were exposed to in-cessant alarms from the pirates of the coast, and to still greater dangers from the sea. Our ship was cast among the shoals by the violence of the tempest, and drifted along for miles, ploughing the sands with its rudder. If, as we dreaded each moment, any hidden rock or sunken reef had lain in our course, we must inevitably have been wrecked, and have perished, every soul. I witnessed many tears on this occasion, much anguish and lamentation when death seemed very near. Nevertheless, God willed not our loss, but to enlighten our minds by present danger that we might know from experience our mortal frailty whenever we should be tempted to lean upon any human devices. When we are convinced once for all of the impotence of our own efforts and have withdrawn our confidence from all earthly powers, to rest it unshaken in the sovereign Arbiter of the world, Who can, in one moment, turn aside the dangers we have encountered for His sake; then we know indeed that the universe is ruled by the hand of Providence, and that our very lives are of little worth beside the heavenly happiness which is prepared for us. Truly, one cannot fear death, possessing such consolations. And when the peril is past, though words fail most strangely to express our feelings, there remains a soothing sense of divine protection which prompts us day and night to accept gladly, to suffer patiently, every trial for the love of our dear Lord. The thought of Him commands our lifelong homage. It is from His infinite goodness alone that we derive strength and courage to serve Him faithfully.

"The Moluccas are composed of a great number of little islands, but whether any part belongs to the mainland, is not yet certainly known. The inhabitants (for most of them are peopled) dwell in big villages, and would willingly turn towards Christianity, were there any to exhort them thereto. Had we but one of the houses of our Company here, the greater part of the people would be won over to the faith of Jesus. Foreseeing this, I have made a vow to compass the establishment of the same for our brethren. The Pagans, in this island of Amboyna, are much more numerous than the Mahometans, the two races being kept apart by a deep-rooted hostility. The latter, in fact, tyrannise over the former, compelling them either to worship the Prophet, or to become the slaves of his followers; nevertheless, for the most part, they abhor the name of Mahomet even more than the yoke of bondage, and reject the Moslem superstition. The name of our Lord is less distasteful to these oppressed ones, nor are they so far removed but that they might be drawn to Him, would any man call them into His flock. It is now seventy years since the venom of Mahometanism was first spread amidst these simple Pagans. Certain priests, called Kacis, from Mecca, the city of Arabia where the body of the execrable impostor is still kept with great veneration, penetrated hither, and led many of the people into their errors. Since, however, they have left them quite ignorant and unlearned in the doctrine they profess, I hope to banish it without difficulty.

"I communicate all these details that you may share my concern, and experience some natural regret at the loss of so many souls, for the mere want of Christian aid. Let those who come to help us, lose no time. Know they ever so little of literature or science, they will be capable of the ministry here, provided only that they come filled with noble ardour, to spend their lives and to breathe their last sigh amidst these people for Jesus' sake. Came there in this spirit but twelve men every year, the hateful sect of Mahomet were speedily annihilated, and all the people brought to Christ. . . . .

" There are islands, too, amidst these seas where they feed upon human flesh, that of prisoners taken in war, principally. Of such as die a natural death, they do not touch the bodies, but cut off the hands and feet as a delicacy. Nay, if certain stories are to be credited, they carry barbarity to such a point, that one desiring to make a great feast, will demand of his neighbour an aged parent, to be slaughtered and devoured, promising to accommodate him with a like victim on a future occasion. Next month, nevertheless, I go to visit an island where the dreadful crime of cannibalism is of the most frequent occurrence. I do so because of a rumour that the aborigines are minded to forsake their sinful and detestable practices, and to conform themselves to the sanctity of the Christian code.

" These isles are favoured with the brightest skies, covered with tall and noble trees, watered by abundant showers, protected on every side with high cliffs and natural ramparts, so that on the approach of an enemy the inhabitants have only to retreat behind the bristling rocks, to find themselves secure from attack, with neither need nor use for artificial defences. There are, however, frequent earthquakes in these parts, of so great violence that ships in the

shallow seas are struck as it were upon a rock, the
ground heaves with terrible noises, and every mortal
is seized with unspeakable horror.   Many of the islets
also emit flames, and belch forth subterranean fires
on every side, with such fury that no brass cannon
of whatsoever magnitude casts forth projectiles with
the like force.   Often great masses of rock are flung
to a distance by these explosions.   It seems, if I
may so speak, that God has here opened for a little
space the very gates of hell, that these creatures, to
whom none have foretold the punishment destined
for the wicked, may perceive, as in a vision, the
fiery furnace wherein the souls of sinners are
eventually to be consumed, so that the horror of the
scene may warn them, and enable them at least to
realise the torments that await them if they shun not
the abysses of crime and infamy.

"A different language prevails in every island.
The idioms are various, and the dwellers, even in
neighbouring villages, speak not with the same
accent; nevertheless, for convenience of trade, the
Malay tongue is well-nigh universal.   Therefore,
when I was at Malacca, I busied myself in translating
into that language the Apostles' Creed, with the
explanation of the sign of the cross, the formula of

General Confession, the Lord's Prayer, the Angelic Salutation, and the Ten Commandments, so as to make my speech intelligible to the people, at least upon these high subjects.

" The Malays have scarcely any written records ; only a few of them know how to read or write, and these use the Arabic character taught them by the false priests of Mahomet."

Later he writes from the island of Moro :

" There are here many Christian villages long deprived of religious culture by reason of the distance from the Indies ; the barbarians also having put to death the single priest who had come to dwell among them. I baptized great numbers of infants, and in the space of three months visited all the communities and brought them again into subjection to the truths I proclaimed in the Lord Jesus. These islands are full of perils, the inhabitants being ever at war among themselves, barbarous and ignorant, without record of the past or any knowledge of letters. They destroy their enemies by poison, and great numbers of them perish by that death. The land is barren, without vines or corn, and fresh water exceedingly scarce. . . . .

" I give you these details, beloved brethren, that ye

may also understand the measure of spiritual gladness with which the soul is overwhelmed in these
wildernesses. All dangers, all trials borne for the
love of our Saviour Jesus Christ, become abundant
treasures of divine consolation, so that after a few
years in these islands our eyes might seem as
strangers to the light of day by reason of incessant
yet most blessed tears. Nowhere do I remember
to have entertained more lively or durable impressions of spiritual joys, nowhere have I borne
so lightly bodily fatigue and suffering than here,
surrounded by open enemies and doubtful friends,
cut off from all succour in time of sickness; nay,
even from things most necessary to existence.
Truly, according to my experience, those islands
should bear the name of heavenly hope, rather than
that of fearful death."

It is related of Xavier, that while celebrating Mass
at Moro, in a hut he had built for the purpose on
the sides of the volcano, the mountain threw up
wreaths of flame to heaven, and the earth tottered
under his feet, and the building shook to its base;
the terrified worshippers fled, but Xavier, standing
in meek composure before the rocking altar, deli-

berately completed the mysterious sacrifice, rejoicing, as he tells us, that the demons of the island then winged their flight before the presence of Christ.

There does not seem to have ever been any intention on Xavier's part of remaining in these islands. He only went to test the possibility of doing so, to show the way to spirits less daring than himself. " God forbid " (he said to one questioning the expediency of his constant journeyings) " that I should risk other men's lives in any place where I had not first ventured my own, or desire my fellows to do aught that I had not myself tried."

CHAPTER XII

INDIA, 1548

" Thine to work as well as pray,
Clearing thorny wrongs away ;
Plucking up the weeds of sin,
Letting heaven's warm sunshine in."
WHITTIER.

" Salvation ! oh, salvation!
The joyful sound proclaim,
Till each remotest nation
Has heard Messiah's name."
HEBER.

Two years of stirring adventure were succeeded by one of comparative calm, devoted by the indefatigable missionary to righting all that had gone wrong in his absence—in fact, to a general supervision and settlement of the affairs of the Society throughout the Indies. His work consisted in revisiting the churches and colleges already founded on the western coast and promoting the establishment of others; in despatching, to those places where the services were most needful, the members of his Order who now began to come after him in answer to his reiterated summons; and in diligently collecting information about newly discovered lands, especially the islands of Japan, destined to be henceforth associated with his memory. On the 20th of January, 1548, he reports himself safely returned to Cochin, the central station of Western India. How short a time was afforded to repose after the fatiguing voyage from Malacca, may be inferred from the fact that four important letters bear date of the very day after his arrival. From one of these, addressed to the brethren at Rome, we gather many of the particulars recorded in the preceding chapter, and learn also the fair measure of success that had attended his preaching.

"I have good cause," he writes, "to thank God for the fruit of these labours. Our converts in the Moluccas are so filled with ardour that they are continually chanting the praise and glory of God. The children in the market-place, the young maidens and wives within their houses, the labourer in the fields, the fisherman upon the waters, all rehearse in their songs the blessed truths of Christianity; and the

words of their hymns being in the native tongue,
are intelligible alike to the new Christians and their
unconverted neighbours. Finally, the Lord permitted that the Portuguese of the country as well
as all the other inhabitants conceived, in a little
while, some friendship for me, so that I seemed to
have found favour in their eyes.

"On my return to the Moluccas about the season
of Lent, the greater part of the native wives of the
Portuguese residents became partakers of the holy
Sacrament, which they had never before in their
lives been bidden to approach. Also during the six
months I remained in those parts, the Europeans
there, as well as their women and children and the
native Christians, made great progress in piety.
When, at the end of Lent, I desired to sail again
for Malacca, I received the most touching proofs of
affection, not only from the faithful, but likewise from
unbelievers. I sought to embark secretly by night,
to escape the tears and lamentations of my beloved
flock, but my departure could not be concealed, and
I found myself overtaken by my friends. This
sorrowful parting in the darkness of the night with
the children whom I had, as it were, born to the
Lord, was very bitter to my soul, and I feared

greatly lest my absence should affect their welfare. I exhorted them every one to recite diligently each day at the same hour the Catechism, and to commit to memory the short explanation of the holy symbol which I had prepared for their use. A worthy priest, and good friend of mine, has undertaken the charge of instructing them for two hours daily, and teaching once a week the articles of faith to the wives of the Portuguese, also of preaching to them on the Sacraments of Penance and the Eucharist.

"In 1546, I had written from Amboyna to the brethren newly arrived from Portugal, that they should take advantage the following year, of some vessel sailing from the Indies to Malacca, and follow me thither. This they have now done. Thus, of the Company (two of their number, Jean de Biera and Minez Ribiero, being priests duly ordained), arrived most fortunately just as I reached Malacca, on my homeward way. We dwelt there together for a month to my great satisfaction, for I doubt not they will now be capable of rendering the greatest service to the cause of religion in the Moluccas, whither they departed in August. Whilst we tarried thus at Malacca, I made them acquainted with the ways of the countries I had visited, and gave them the

light of my experience as to the best manner
of dealing with the inhabitants.   Their abode will
be so distant that we may hardly expect to receive from them one letter in the year.   I have
desired them therefore to make report to Rome also
every year of the progress of religion in those
countries and their prospects for the future.   This
they have faithfully promised me to do.

" Nor were the four months of my sojourn at
Malacca, awaiting a favourable opportunity to pass
on to India, otherwise void of religious occupation.
Indeed, as I could not by myself satisfy all who
needed holy services, it was not possible altogether
to avoid giving offence ; nevertheless, such slight
discontent, having its root in softened and expectant
feeling, gave me no concern, but rather comfort, as
proving increase of piety.   Much of my time was
devoted to overcoming and reconciling the quarrels
and hatreds that uprise so frequently among the
Portuguese, always a warlike people. . . . .

" Most earnestly have I commended that congregation to the care of a secular priest.   He is to take
my place among them, to celebrate the same services,
to follow the same order of daily instruction; and I
trust that, by God's grace, he may be enabled to per-

form his promise without hindrance. The chief
citizens of Malacca entreated me when I was leaving
their town to send thither with all speed two
members of our Company, that the divine Word
might be continually proclaimed to them, their wives
and neighbours, nor their children and servants lack
such instructions as I had given in religious doctrine.
This claim was urged with so much ardour that I perceive it to be my solemn duty to forward zealously
the pious desire to men who have indeed deserved
well at our hands."

During Xavier's sojourn at Malacca, Alareddin,
a Mahometan chief of Sumatra, laid siege to the
town, which prepared to capitulate, but before
this was accomplished Father Francis came into
the harbour in his little weather-beaten boat.
With all the fire of his Spanish blood he called
upon the subjects of the most faithful King not to
put the foul scorn upon themselves of yielding to
their barbaric enemies. He took the command, ordered seven of the ships to be equipped for sea; he
animated the crews with promises of both temporal
and eternal triumphs, and despatched them to meet
and conquer the enemy. The flotilla sailed, but a
sudden tempest drove it out to sea. Day after day

passed without intelligence, and rumours of defeat were rife. Xavier's name was repeated from mouth to mouth with cries of vengeance. The excited populace sought him, and he was found kneeling before the altar. On a sudden he raised aloft his crucifix, and with deep emotion breathed a prayer for victory. A solemn pause ensued, and after a brief but agonising silence he bounded to his feet, and with a clear and ringing voice he cried : "Christ has conquered for us ! we shall see our fleet again."

It came, but amid the shouts of triumph and adoring gratitude, the Saint turned away and retraced his toilsome way to the shores of the Indian peninsula. After his return to Goa he writes the following striking epistle to Diego di Pereira, Ambassador from the King of Portugal to China :

" May the grace and love of our Lord Jesus Christ be ever with you for your comfort and salvation.

"I would gladly have seen you before your departure for China in place of simply writing to you, but the Viceroy has bidden me hither to Goa, and it seemed my duty to obey his wish. I had designed to visit my brethren on the Comorin coasts, and had likewise hoped to meet with you, my excellent friend, and hold counsel with you concerning the plan I have conceived of going to Japan. Next year I shall not fail to execute the same, for I am now well assured that in that country we shall find an abundant harvest for the Lord, and be enabled to propagate the faith of Christ.

"In the name of our friendship I counsel you, before departing for China, to secure the treasure of inestimable price so frequently neglected by merchants—that is, a good conscience—a thing of which many of them scarcely acknowledge the existence. They are all persuaded that the care of their soul or their conscience would be the infallible cause of their ruin. Nevertheless, I trust that with the divine aid, my worthy friend Diego di Pereira may furnish himself with the priceless pearl, nor fail to prosper in his calling, whilst others, regardless of spiritual riches, may fall, perhaps, into grievous poverty. I will not cease to pray the Lord that He may give you good speed in China, and bring you back to us in health and safety, richer even in grace than in goods. . . . .

"May the Lord Jesus Christ abide with you, as I pray that He may be with me likewise.

                                                      "FRANCIS.

"GOA, *April 2nd,* 1548."

To Loyola he writes :

"How great were the perils of my voyage from
Malacca hitherward! For three days and three
nights our barque seemed the plaything of a tempest,
such as I never before witnessed. Many on board
were weeping at the near prospect of death, or
making vows nevermore to approach the sea, if, by
Heaven's help, they were at this time spared. The
traders were fain to purchase their lives by abandon-
ing their goods to the devouring waves. While the
storm was at the worst, I entreated the Lord through
the potent intercessions of our spiritual friends, and
of all faithful Christians, appealing by the Church,
the Spouse of Christ, whose supplications ascend
continually from her earthly exile to the gates of
Heaven, for the protection of the Almighty in our
evil strait. . . . .

"It seems to me that I am oftentimes shown
inwardly of the Lord the countless bodily risks and
spiritual failings from which I have been preserved
for the sake of my brethren, striving upon my behalf
while here below, nor forgetting me amidst the joys
of Heaven. And these words of mine, Fathers and
brothers beloved in the Lord Jesus, are my confession
to you of the immeasurable benefits I owe to God

and to you; for truly I have no power to repay either.

"I know not how to stop, when once I begin to write concerning our Company; yet the speedy departure of our ships warns me to make an end of my letter, nor can I do it otherwise than by this solemn declaration :—' When I forget thee, O Brotherhood of Jesus ! let my right hand forget its cunning.' "

CHAPTER XIII

JAPAN

" Those whom Thy Spirit's dread vocation severs,
   To lead the vanguard of Thy conquering host,
   Whose toilsome years are spent in brave endeavours
   To bear Thy saving name from coast to coast."
                                    HYMNS A. & M.

AT Malacca, Francis Xavier, holding himself in devout readiness to follow the divine guidance he continually implored, received a call, scarcely less doubtful than that of the Apostle to the Gentile world of old, who " beheld a man of Macedonia saying, ' Come over and help us.' "

"About the month of April, 1547," he writes to the brethren in Europe, " I fell in with a Portuguese merchant, a man of exceeding piety and veracity, who talked to me unceasingly of the great islands of Japan, lately discovered. It seems that the Christian religion might prosper better there than in any other region of the Indies, since the people are of inquiring minds and eager for enlightenment beyond any upon earth. This merchant was accompanied by a Japanese named Auger, who after certain conversations with persons from Malacca was moved within himself to come and seek me out. He had held counsel with his friends among the Portuguese trading at Japan, revealing to them the uneasiness of his conscience, asking of them some means to save his soul, and turn away the wrath of God. These men brought him forthwith in their ship to Malacca, but I, alas! was then absent at the Moluccas, and he turned sorrowfully towards his own land again. Already was he within sight of it, when a sudden tempest arose and drove him back to us without grave peril. Then he learned of my return and came to meet me, earnestly craving religious instruction. He is partially acquainted with the Portuguese tongue, so that we understood each other without an interpreter; and if all his countrymen have the like thirst of knowledge they, must exceed in intelligence any nation hitherto discovered. Being present at the Catechism meeting, he carefully wrote down in a book the

articles of faith.   In the church, before all the people,
he recited from memory the lessons he had learned,
asking numberless questions with great acuteness.
His desire of learning is inordinate, and what can
be a more powerful aid to the understanding of
truth ?   The eighth day after his arrival at Malacca
he sailed for India.   I would have had him in the
vessel with myself, but the ties that bound him to
others making the same voyage, permitted him not
to separate from the true friends who had already
done him so great service.   I now look for him to
join me at Cochin ere ten days be past.

"I inquired of this Auger whether, should I indeed
return with him to Japan, he considered it probable
that the Christian religion would be accepted there.
He made answer, that his countrymen were not
wont to give immediate assent to all that was pro-
pounded to them, but that they would question me
so as thoroughly to understand the dogmas I
brought, and would watch very closely whether
my actions accorded in every case with my words.
Could I satisfy them in these respects, both
appeasing their reasonable curiosity by conclusive
arguments, and showing myself pure and blameless in life, he doubted not their instruction and

enlightenment would speedily follow, bringing to the faith King and Court and citizens, since it is the character of this people to obey the dictates of reason.

"My friend the Portuguese merchant, who had passed some time in Japan, has left me notes, collected with much care, descriptive of the country and the manners of the inhabitants, with details of such things as he has himself seen, or heard from credible witnesses. These papers I forward to you with my letter.

"I have a secret conviction that within two years either I, or some other member of our Company, must go to Japan. This Auger will by that time have perfectly mastered our language. He will have witnessed the power of the Portuguese in the Indies, and perceived the advantages of European industry and civilised life. He will have prepared himself worthily for baptism, and will have helped me in translating into Japanese the Catechism and the history of our Lord, if, as I trust, he possess the art of writing the language of his country.

"All our merchants from Japan assure me that in proceeding thither I should do far better than by remaining in the Indies ; that I should, in fact, find myself at once in friendly relations with men of understanding, and of a teachable spirit. It is true that the voyage is beset with danger, from the terrible storms that prevail in these seas, no less than from the Chinese pirates, and many vessels are lost by the way. Nevertheless, I expect much, fathers and brothers well-beloved, from your prayers to the Lord for our deliverance, in circumstances that might prove fatal to others."

His next letters to Rome reveal to us some melancholy convictions now matured in the writer's thoughts, while they also touch on the new schemes that were springing from the grave of former hopes.

" O my only Father in Jesus Christ," he addresses Ignatius. " Doubtless you have already learned from communications lately forwarded to Rome by our brethren here, what precious fruits have been gathered in these lands by God's mercy and with the benefit of your prayers. There remains to me the duty of making you acquainted with the actual condition of countries so far removed from the metropolis of the world.

"The Indian races, so far as I have been able to judge, are totally savage, and can only be attracted by discourses flattering to their barbarous nature. They are mostly indifferent to the knowledge of truth and salvation, and opposed to virtue by perverse dispositions ; unstable in the extreme, of little faith, and of no energy—brought up in lying and wickedness. These are the people we are striving to turn into Christians ! Think what it must be to labour amongst men, who neither know God nor give heed to reason, but rebel against the voice calling them to forsake sins that have grown a part of their nature ! Have not we, your sons, an especial claim on your care, a right to continual remembrance in your petitions ?

"You can imagine the difficulties of teaching men who know not God and rebel against reason—who rise in indignation against the friend who calls them to forsake their sins, and cling to the false gods who do not curb their pleasures.

"The human frame is sorely tried in these climates by the burning heats of summer and the bitter winds that prevail in the rainy season. Food and all the

L

necessaries of life are scarce, whilst the labour both of mind and body in dealing with men of this nature is immense. I may add that the languages of these countries are most difficult to acquire, and the dangers to which we are exposed are countless. Nevertheless, let the Company of Jesus thank the Lord on our behalf, for I can declare that all your children in India have been mercifully preserved in body and in soul. We have won also the good graces of our countrymen and of the natives, so that the goodwill borne to us moves all men to wonder.

" According to my experience, all the Indians are profoundly ignorant. It follows that those who are sent to preach the Gospel to them have less need of science than of virtue, of learning than of charity. Patience, obedience, purity amidst endless temptations, vigour both of mind and body, are the qualities our brethren here require. I speak in this way that selection may be made of these sent to us, that they may be proved when possible, and that only men of pure lives and humble minds may be sent to us.

" The Rector whom you send to direct the college of Goa should possess two principal qualities ; he should be able to obey and to conciliate—to win by gentleness and humility the goodwill of all.

" Let him not attempt to govern the brethren under him by severity as if they were slaves. Such rigorous treatment would cause many to leave the Society and few to enter it. In my opinion, no person ought to be retained among us against his wish. I would permit, nay enforce, the departure of all to whom the rule of our order is irksome ; treating with tenderness and regard those who are suited to their profession, that we may keep them with us and give them opportunity to exist in grace and virtue through the trials that await them here in the service of our Lord. The Fraternity of Jesus is in truth the fraternity of love and union ; severity and servile fear must be banished from it.

" My knowledge of this country permits me to have no hope that our Society can be perpetuated through the natives. Hardly could the Christian religion survive were we and our fellows withdrawn ; it is necessary therefore to send us new men for every part of India where there are any Christians. Our brethren are now to be found, four at the Moluccas, two at Malacca, six at Cape

Comorin, two at Contam, two at Barciam, four at
Socotra. These places are very different from each
other. The Moluccas, more than a thousand miles
from Goa, Malacca five hundred, and the nearest,
Contam, one hundred and twenty miles distant.

" You must understand that the Portuguese are
masters only of the Indian coast, possessing but
a few fortified places inland. The indigenous population seem so delivered over to sin that we have
small hope of seeing many of them become Christians ;
nay, the very proposal of such a thing is taken as an
insult, and all our care is to try and hold fast the
few converts we have already made. If some consideration were shown there we might do better, but
the sight of the contempt with which our converts are
treated by the Portuguese, makes the natives refuse
to enter our churches or listen to our teaching.

" My labours therefore become less profitable
here, while I know that Japan, a country beyond
China, is entirely peopled by infidels thirsting for
knowledge.

" Shall I not go thither ? I would undertake the
voyage rejoicing in the Spirit with unspeakable hope,
looking forward to an abundant and lasting harvest
among that people.

"At the college of Goa there are now three Japanese students, who returned with me from Malacca last April. They give marvellous accounts of their country. They are young men of irreproachable conduct and lively intelligence, especially Paul (Auger), who addresses a long letter to you. In the space of eight months he has learned to read and write in Portuguese. He is now exercising himself with great profit in spiritual meditations. He is well instructed in the mysteries of the Christian religion, and I trust, by God's grace, he will be the means of making many Christians in Japan. Immediately upon my arrival I purpose presenting myself to the sovereign, and afterwards making my way to the colleges and universities, where I shall doubtless find an abundance of hearers, according to the statement of this Paul. The Japanese take their religious doctrine from the University of Cenic, a city beyond China and Cathay, a journey of a year and a half from Goa, where I shall be able to obtain for you some more definite information concerning the customs and literature of the nation. The doctrines and statutes of this university, I am told, are recognised throughout China and Cathay, so I shall not neglect to send an account of it to the University

of Paris, that the universities may be advised of our
discovery.

" I take with me on this expedition but one.
European, Cosmo de Torres, the Andalusian, who has
joined our Company here. The three young Japanese
of whom I have told you accompany me, and about
next April, if the Lord permits, we shall set out.
Japan is more than thirteen hundred miles from Goa,
by the way of Malacca and China. The voyage
is said to be so unsafe, on account of sudden storms
and hidden reefs as well as pirates, that it is considered fortunate when one of two vessels reaches
its destination.

" Notwithstanding this, I am filled with the utmost
happiness at the thought of this enterprise, nor
could I think it right, were I forewarned of worse
perils, to shrink from the labour put before me. The
discourses of the Japanese Paul, nay rather, the
thoughts that Heaven has raised within my soul, fill
me with hope that this journey is for the advancement of the Christian faith.

" The enclosed letter from Paul will sufficiently
show you the facilities which this great empire presents for the sowing of the Gospel seed.

" There are in the Indies about fifteen places

where houses for our Society might be established if the King could be induced to assign for the purpose funds from his Treasury. I have myself addressed his Majesty on the subject. I have likewise communicated with Simon Rodriguez, and have shown him how greatly it might advance religious interests were he himself with your consent to come hither, bringing a goodly band of our brethren, and above all a powerful reinforcement of preachers ; supported by royal authority he might be instrumental in founding many colleges of our order.

"O Father! trust me in this matter. The favour that Simon enjoys would make his coming most seasonable to our cause. He would be armed with power from the King to establish colleges, to protect both existing Christians and the natives who would be converted if assured of safety. I pray you to encourage him with your approval. Antonio Gomez assures me that it is Father Simon's full intention to come to the Indies with a great party of followers from the college at Coimbra. Are there not plenty both at home and elsewhere who have neither talent for preaching nor great learning, yet who might do good service to religion, if only they had some experience of the world, and among other virtues necessary for the ministry in heathen lands, the gift of chastity, and the strength of mind and body to undertake the heavy labours that will here fall to their share ?

" You would be doing a good work, and I think a pleasure to the Lord, were you to send to all members of the Company living in the Indies a letter of spiritual direction which would be to us a testament where you bestow on us, the last of your children and exiled from your presence, the riches of the heavenly blessing you have received from above.

"I ask of you but one favour on my account, which is, that some priest of our Company would celebrate a monthly Mass for me in the chapel of St. Peter's in the Janiculum, at the place where the Apostle was crucified. You might likewise charge one of the Fathers to write to us concerning the Company, to tell us who have lately made profession and to keep us acquainted with the labours and triumphs of the brethren.

" I have arranged that my letters should be sent from Goa to Malacca, and at Malacca they are to be transcribed, and copies forwarded by different routes to Japan.

"Finally, O Father of my soul! most venerable

in my eyes of all mankind, I beseech you on my knees as I indite these words, cease not to implore the Lord that so long as my life shall last, He will grant me knowledge of His most holy will and strength to perform the same.

" COCHIN, 14*th January*, 1549."

The next letter is to the Simon Rodriguez spoken of in the preceding pages :

" I cannot express in words, oh, my dearly beloved Simon, what joy I felt on the arrival of Antonio Gomez and his company. We have sore need of help here and in the city of Ormuz and at the fortress of Din, and I have decided on despatching Antonio to Ormuz, where his gift of eloquence and general capacity will find full scope.

" It were indeed meritorious in the sight of God should you yourself hasten to the Indies, bringing with you some brethren of experience and wisdom. It is not deep science that will convert the infidels. The people here are barbarous and uncultured, so that even unlearned men of steadfast virtue and robust health may do great good in advancing God's kingdom. In whatever place throughout the Indies we can have a preacher of the Company, with a brother to assist him in the ministry, there may be established a residence to direct the education both of Portuguese and native children.

" I have written to Father Ignatius asking him to authorise your coming, and likewise to the King praying him to send you to the Indies, with many followers and much authority, for in truth your presence here might be most beneficial to us all. Another object of my letter to his Majesty was to commend to him the Portuguese orphans whose parents, dying in his service, have left their children alone and unprovided for. They do not even receive the arrears of their fathers' pay, and it surely were a useful work to found homes where these might be well brought up and instructed in all good works. Nor have the native children less claim upon his Majesty, and it would be well if these could be taught the Catechism of our faith by the King's command. Some money has already been assigned for these purposes at the prayer of Miguel Vaz, former Vicar-General of the Indies, but it is not by any means sufficient.

" I have recently obtained information about the empire of Japan, situated more than six hundred miles beyond China. The inhabitants, I am told,

have subtle minds and long for instruction of all
kinds. All Portuguese returning from thence tell the
same tale, and it is confirmed by some Japanese, who
last year followed me from Malacca to India, and
who are now being initiated into our sacred mysteries in the college at Goa. I have already told
you Paul's account of his life, and after hearing his
story I have resolved to go to Japan next April, as I
am convinced that the Christian religion will make
marvellous progress in that country. Also, I begin
to feel idle here ; our fraternity can do all that is
now needed, and when you come, and I shall have
verified the statements of the Japanese, I shall ask
of you that you will favour our expedition to Japan.
After that I trust, with the assistance of God, that
some of our members will penetrate into China, and
from China to the celebrated University of Cenic,
situated beyond China and Cathay.

"According to the recitals of Paul, the Japanese,
the Chinese, and all the Tartars are initiated into the
priesthood at this university. The religious doctrines of the Japanese are contained in sacred books,
kept secret and written in a language unknown to
the people, so that Paul, being an unlettered man,
could give us no information about the religion of his

country. When I go to that country I will, if it please God, write to you in great detail as to what the sacred books of Japan contain.

" I have resolved, immediately on my arrival, that I will present myself to the sovereign and to the heads of the principal colleges, and write all that I hear, not only to my brothers in India, but to the universities of Portugal and Italy, so as to show that learning and science still fail to save infidels from perdition.

"We have been told a serious accident has befallen Francis Perez at the Isle of Moro, but no letter from him or news worthy of belief confirms the statement. Still it is very certain that those who are there are proved in the furnace. Indeed, I know no place in the world that those seeking the honour of God and the salvation of souls are in such mortal danger as in the Isle of Moro. Pray God for those who are there and for those who will follow them, for I am persuaded that soon this island will no longer be known as the Isle of Moro, but the Isle of Martyrs.

" The voyage to Japan seems filled with difficulties and dangers, but I hope in two months to make proof of them, and that, with the permission of God, when you arrive in India you will receive a letter from me from Japan.

"I cease to write to-day, though it seems to me that I take such pleasure in it that I know not how to stop. I hope one day we may meet again, be it in China, in Japan, or at any rate in Heaven—in the Heaven where, called together by the gracious and infinite beneficence of God, we shall rejoice through eternity in the delight of dwelling in the sight of the supreme source of all blessings. Amen."

Xavier left India, as he proposed, in April 1549, taking with him one priest, one lay companion and three Japanese neophytes. These last had been given instruction in the essentials of salvation, and had been baptised at Goa. They also understood Portuguese as well as their native language, and so could act as interpreters, and they were filled with the most enthusiastic desire to carry the holy faith to their benighted brothers.

In May the party reached Malacca, where Xavier received letters from Portuguese merchants in Japan, telling him that a prince of that country wished to become a Christian, and that he had sent to ask the

Viceroy of India to send a mission to instruct him and his people in the knowledge of Jesus Christ. The merchants also stated that on their arrival in Japan they had been lodged in a house infested by demons, but that by placing crosses about the house the demons ceased to trouble them.

The letters also added that Japan offered a vast field for the preaching of the Gospel, that its people were learned and always anxious to listen to anything new, so Xavier writes :

" I conceive if we have divine support, we have a hope of gathering an immense harvest for God, and of seeing a vast crowd of erring souls brought into the bosom of the Church. God grant that our weakness and sinfulness do not stand in the way of our being ministers to His glory.

" The Japanese with us have forewarned us that the Bonzes (Japanese priests) would be scandalised if they saw us eat fish or meat, so we are resolved to an absolute abstinence in this matter, so as to offend no one. We also learn that there are an infinite number of these Bonzes who live a very austere life and exercise a great influence over all classes of society. I tell you this to show you how great need we have of your prayers and those of all good Christians to help us in our desperate fight. We intend to leave Malacca on St. John's Day. We hope to see from the sea the famous empire of China, but we shall not try to approach its shores. Our sailors expect that we shall arrive in Japan about the middle of August."

The party left Malacca as arranged, the governor helping them by ordering that a Chinese junk should take them straight to their destination, and by providing them with all necessaries for their journey, and with handsome presents to be given to the authorities in Japan, in order that they might be favourable to the preaching of the Gospel.

Xavier reached Japan safely in August 1549, having had a fair wind, but having suffered much because the Chinese captain of their boat would sacrifice to an idol on board ship, notwithstanding all their efforts to convert him from the error of his ways, and would consult the demon of this idol upon all subjects, even as to whether or no he should safely bring the Saint and his companions to Japan!

However, after some delays they arrived at Cangoxima, the capital and port of the kingdom of

Satsuma, which was the country of Paul, one of the Japanese returning with Xavier. The travellers were there received with affectionate welcome by the friends of Paul and by other inhabitants of the town. Xavier, in writing to Coimbra, thus gives his first impressions of this people. He says :

" The people we have encountered here surpass in moral qualities all people discovered up to this time. I think there cannot exist a nation superior to the Japanese in natural gifts. Their intelligence is bright and open, and they prefer honour to all other gifts. They are for the most part poor, but poverty dishonours no one; they carry this opinion to an extent that would shame many Christian people. The nobles without fortune have as much consideration as those that are opulent. The people give much honour to the nobles, and the nobles to the princes and kings, holding it a great honour to obey their slightest word; and this not from fear, but because it was the course of conduct required by their own dignity. They are sober and moderate in their living, but indulge rather too freely in their wine made from rice. They mostly know how to write, which will be a great help to us in teaching them religion. They have only one wife. They are marvellously disposed for all that is good, and listen with avidity to discourses on God and holy things. They readily lend an ear to discourses that conform to nature and reason, and if you can show them that any of their faults are against reason, they are ready to follow the dictates of their own intelligence."

Of the priests, the Bonzes, Xavier speaks no good word. He says their discipline is lax and their life extremely disorderly, and that with this they have great influence, which is bad for the people. He discoursed with many of them, but found them full of uncertainty. He was friendly with their chiefs, who were loud in admiration for their daring in coming from Portugal across the seas to bring them a new religion. He still believed that the land was longing for the news of Christ, and wonderfully ready for conversion. The Prince of Cangoxima received them with great honour, and gave his people permission to embrace the Christian religion if they wished.

The high hopes with which Xavier ended the year 1549 were a little clouded by the end of the next year, when he writes to Goa as follows :

M

" My beloved Brethren—

"I wrote to you last year from Cangoxima about our journey to and our arrival at Japan, and I told you what works Jesus Christ had deigned to do through us. I told you how we reached the country of our dear brother Paul, and how well we were received by his family and friends ; how Paul converted them for the most part, and we received them into the flock of the Lord Jesus ; how we remained over a year in the same place, and over a hundred persons were there made Christians, none of their friends or relatives making any objection. Seeing our success, the Bonzes, however, went to the king of that part of Japan (Satsuma), and declared to him that if he allowed his people to embrace the religion of Jesus Christ, his power would be despised. They persuaded him that the law of the new God was in direct opposition to the law of Japan, that the followers of Christ would deny the authority of the ancient lawgivers, and that the result would be to ruin the national constitution and his own power. They urged him to declare for the old legislators, and to order without delay that it should be death to any one in the future to become a Christian. The prince, persuaded by their words, issued the desired edict. In the meantime we had written a book which contained the essential articles of the Christian faith. This we had translated into Japanese, and put into the hands of those who desired to become Christians, and we found our converts take an extreme satisfaction in it. They recognised the evidence of the truth of Christianity, and the falsehood of their own religion, but none would embrace the religion of Jesus Christ for fear of their prince.

"Towards the end of this year (1550), seeing how we were opposed in the propagation of our religion, we resolved to pass on to another part of Japan. We took leave of our neophytes, who were grieved to see us go, though deeply grateful to us for having made such sacrifices to come and teach them the way of salvation. We left among them our dear brother Paul to continue to enlighten all the newly converted in the articles of the true religion.

"After some days' journeying we arrived at Amangachi (capital of the kingdom of Wangato), a town of more than ten thousand families, and there we found many persons who desired to be instructed in the religion of Jesus Christ. We resolved to preach two days a week in their public places, and we read aloud our book. Some of the nobles called us into their houses to instruct them, and they told us that if our religion seemed preferable to their own they would not hesitate to change at once. Others tried to turn us into ridicule, following us into the streets with insulting cries and jeers at our teaching and religion.

" After some days the king called us before him and asked whence we came, and why we came to Japan. We answered that we were Europeans, sent to Japan to preach the religion of the true God and his Son, Jesus Christ, without whom no one could be saved. The prince invited us to explain these mysteries to him, and we read him part of our book. He listened with extreme attention for an hour and then dismissed us. We preached in the public places for many days, and were listened to with much attention, but the number of our converts was few.

" There seemed so little fruit of our efforts in this place that we moved on to Miaco, which is the most considerable town in Japan. This journey took us two months, and we suffered many dangers from the war which was raging on our route, to say nothing of the rigour of the climate and the brigands that infested the roads. Arrived at Miaco, we waited some days for an audience of the king to ask from him liberty to preach, but we found it impossible to get access to him. Then we thought we would try to touch the hearts of the people and see if we could gather them into the harvest of the Lord. But all the citizens were in arms, and a civil war was going on in the town, so I recognised that circumstances were against the preaching of the Gospel.

" Seeing that Miaco was not peaceful enough for our voices to be heard, we returned to Amangachi and presented to the king, Oxindono, the letters from the Viceroy of India and the Bishop of Goa, and the presents sent by them in token of their friendship. The king was very pleased with the presents, and wished to offer us gold and silver in return. Sending back his gift, we prayed him to give us leave to spread the knowledge of our divine Master in his country, and to give leave to his subjects to listen to us.

" He granted our prayer, and issued an edict that all who desired it were at liberty to embrace the new religion, and he gave us an empty priest-house to live in. A great number of people came to hear about the new religion, and we preached twice a day. We were continually occupied, and such numbers came to hear us that sometimes many were unable to penetrate into our house. Many of our hearers were convinced of the falsehood of their religion and the truth of Christianity, and several came to confess the faith of Jesus Christ.

" The new Christians helped us faithfully by giving us information on the beliefs of the many sects, thereby enabling us to study the arguments wherewith to combat them. In two months we counted about 500 Christians, and the number seemed growing every day."

So writes the Saint in November, 1550. In November, 1551, he quitted Japan, leaving the brothers who accompanied him at Amangachi, where the mission still flourished, though the town passed to another ruler, and there were riots and disturbances of all kinds, about which Xavier writes in full to the brethren in Rome.

However, his share in the work was done, and if the story is true that later missionaries found in Japan 3000 Christians, the names of Cosmo di Torrez and Joam Fernandez, who were left in charge of the mission, should share with Francis Xavier in the glory of their conversion.

CHAPTER XIV

CHINA

" Hold Thou thy Cross before my fading eyes,
  Shine through the gloom, and point me to the skies,
  Heaven's morning breaks and earth's vain shadows flee,
  In life, in death, O Lord, abide with me."

                                        LYTE.

XAVIER left Japan in November, 1551, but he spent some time at Bungo and other stations, and did not arrive at Goa again until the February of 1552. Much time was spent by him in the affairs of his Company, but his letters to Rome show that his next mission was taking shape already in his thoughts. In writing about the details of his Japan mission he says :

" Opposite Japan the immense empire of China lies extended. I am told it enjoys perfect peace, and that it is superior to all Christian kingdoms in the practice of justice and of virtue. The people are clever and fond of learning, their country is rich and beautiful. The Japanese take all their religious belief through the Chinese, and if we can make them embrace the Christian religion, the Japanese will also receive it through them. I hope to go there myself this year (1552), and to penetrate to the sovereign of the empire. China seems so constituted, that if the seed of the Gospel is ever sown it will propagate rapidly. I have a firm hope that God will soon open the gates of China, not only to us, but to all men of zeal and piety, so that all may help in the conversion of erring souls to the truths of salvation.

" I have a little recovered from my journey from Japan, and I hope, through the mercy of God and the infinite merits of the Lord Jesus Christ, that I shall have sufficient bodily strength and spiritual energy to accomplish the laborious journey to China which I desire to make. My hair is white, but I am not weak, and I feel that the conversion of a reasonable people who love truth and justice will bring me supreme consolation."

Again he writes to Simon Rodriguez :

"O my beloved brother, think what an immense work we are inaugurating. If God permit us to carry the light of the Gospel to a people so gentle and docile, you might yourself come to China, there to quench your thirst for the salvation of souls. I feel such a desire to see you again before I die, that I shall now think always that this wish will be realised when China is open."

To the King of Portugal he writes from Goa, 10th April, 1552:

"I wrote to you that I had resolved this year to go to China, where we have the most magnificent hope as to the spread of the Christian faith. In five days I leave Goa for Multana, which is on the road to China, with Diego di Pereira, ambassador to the emperor of that country. We have rich presents, bought by your Majesty's bounty, and we take with us such a gift as never before has been offered by one monarch to another—I mean the Gospel of our Lord Jesus Christ. If the Emperor of China could understand the value of it, he would not hesitate to place it above all his other treasures, however immense these may be. I have a hope that God will have mercy on this vast empire and its inhabitants, and that He will open the eyes of these men, created in His image, to the knowledge of their God and of Jesus Christ, the Saviour of the whole human race.

" We start then, with Pereira, and we will obtain the alliance of the Emperor of China for the King of Portugal, and, above all, we will engage in a war with the devil and all his works. We will signify, first to the sovereign and then to his subjects, in the name of the King of Heaven, that up to this hour they have been worshipping devils, but now they are to worship God the Creator and Jesus the Redeemer.

" It might seem daring to talk of thus imposing doctrines on a powerful sovereign and an infidel people, but we believe ourselves to be inspired by God, who is infinitely more powerful than the Emperor of China, and so we allow no fear nor hesitation to enter our souls."

Some cause prevented his carrying out his plan of going with Diego di Pereira, to whom he writes sorrowfully, entreating him at any rate not to go before him to the Emperor. After a short delay Xavier contrived to get a vessel, and arrived at the island of San Chan, situated about 120 miles from Canton. Thence he hoped to get a passport that would take him to the Emperor, but his hopes seemed likely to be disappointed, and he began to fear that God did not think him worthy of the work. He writes in October to Francis Perez :

" We arrived by the grace of God at San Chan. As soon as possible I had a hut built on the shore, where I celebrated Mass every day, till the fever took me strongly for fifteen days.

" Now God has restored me to health, and I have many holy occupations. I hear confessions, settle quarrels, and serve other offices of our ministry. I cannot, however, yet procure a passage to Canton, all the merchants refuse formally to take me, declaring that it would endanger their goods and their lives, if the governor of the town should hear of it. We still hope to persuade a captain who has only his wife and children on board, to take us to the mainland, as thus there would be no servants to betray him to the governor. If he would land us, I would go straight to the Viceroy and announce that I have come to preach God to the Chinese. I have come here in obedience to the word of God, and He

Who gave to our hearts the thought thus to serve
Him, will preserve us in our dangers.   If God is
our defence, we shall not fail.   Listen to the words
of Christ : ' He that loveth his life, shall lose it ; he
that loseth his life for Me, shall find it ;' which words
are in harmony with the other words of Christ :
' Whoso having put his hand to the plough looketh
back, is not worthy of the Kingdom of Heaven.'   So
in truth we are still resolute to penetrate into China.
May God in His mercy deign to use us to spread
the knowledge of His religion.   ' If God is with us,
who shall be against us ? ' "

The spirit indeed was willing, but still the Saint
could not begin his ministry ; his interpreter failed
him, and still no boat would take him to the mainland.   Almost in despair, he writes : " Fear prevents
these people taking us in their boats to introduce us
into China.   From day to day I wait a merchant
who will arrange with me.   Pray God He will allow
me to carry out my purpose !   If I cannot, I see not
yet my way.   May Jesus Christ give us good
counsel ! "

On the 12th November he writes that he still can

find no boat that will take him to Canton, and that he has resolved to go to Siam and attach himself to the Embassy going to China from thence.

On the 20th of November the fever again attacked him, and those about him witness that he was given to know that the day and hour of his departure drew near, and that God did not intend to give to the Chinese the gift of His salvation through this His servant, who prayed so earnestly that even as prisoner or slave he might be permitted to preach the Gospel among them. But his sickness gained upon him, and in the middle of November he had himself moved on to the vessel which served as hospital to the Portuguese of San Chan. Soon he begged to be again taken to the hut, whence a distant view of China gladdened his eyes. Here he lingered for two weeks, suffering terrible pains, suffering from weakness and from fever, but with peace written upon his wasted features, and joy shining from the eyes that rarely now turned from the Cross of the Master he loved so dearly and had served so well. His wandering words were of God and His mercy; sometimes of regret that China was not suffered to hear the Gospel from his lips ; oftener of grateful thanksgiving to his Saviour for all the mercies

vouchsafed to him. Bowing before the will of his
Heavenly Father, he accepted all as from His hand,
repeating ceaselessly the cry of the leper in the
Gospel, "Jesus, thou Son of David, have mercy
upon me."

On Friday, the 2nd of December, 1552, his earthly
toils and projects ceased for ever. The Angel of
Death appeared with a summons for which, since
death first entered the world, no man was ever more
triumphantly prepared. The agony of the fever still
tortured his feeble frame, but his uplifted crucifix
reminded him of a far more awful woe endured for
his deliverance. His eyes saw blessed ministers of
peace and consolation, and his dying ears heard
strains more beautiful than any he could have
imagined. Tears burst from his eyes, tears of
emotion too great for utterance, and his features
were irradiated as with the first beams of approach-
ing glory; he raised himself on his crucifix, and
crying: "In Thee, Lord, is my hope!" he bowed
his head and died.

*   *   *   *   *   *

The Portuguese among whom he had worked
assembled round his lifeless body, and clothing it in

his canonicals, buried it beside his poor hut, to wait till pious hands should transport it across the sea. Coming to him there was a letter commanding him to return to Europe, in order to be ready to succeed Loyola as head of the Company of Jesus ; but the Saint existed no longer on earth when this evidence of his chief's regard for him reached its destination.

In the next year the remains of Xavier were taken from San Chan, and finally deposited in St. Paul's Church at Goa. He died in the forty-seventh year of his age and the twelfth year of his mission in the East.

"To him belongs the matchless beauty of a human nature in perfect unison with the divine. No man, however abject his condition, hateful his crimes, or disgusting his malady, ever turned to Xavier without learning that there was, at any rate, one human heart that gave him a brother's love To his eyes, the meanest and the lowest, reflected the image of Him whom he followed and adored, nor did he suppose that he could ever serve the Saviour of mankind so acceptably as by ministering to the sorrows of his lost children and recalling them into the way of peace." *

   " Yea, through life, death, through sorrow and through
      sinning,
   He hath sufficed me, and He shall suffice ;
  Christ is the end, for Christ was the beginning,
   Christ the beginning, for the end is Christ." †

---

* "Founders of Jesuitism." FitzJames Stephens.
† "St. Paul." F. W. Myers.

FINIS

Printed by BALLANTYNE, HANSON & Co.
London and Edinburgh

www.ingramcontent.com/pod-product-compliance
Lightning Source LLC
Chambersburg PA
CBHW030537040726

47497CB00008B/2483